THE
DAMNED
SEASON

ALSO BY SHANI STRUTHERS

EVE: A CHRISTMAS
GHOST STORY
(PSYCHIC SURVEYS
PREQUEL)

PSYCHIC SURVEYS
BOOK ONE:
THE HAUNTING OF
HIGHDOWN HALL

PSYCHIC SURVEYS
BOOK TWO:
RISE TO ME

PSYCHIC SURVEYS
BOOK THREE:
44 GILMORE STREET

PSYCHIC SURVEYS
BOOK FOUR:
OLD CROSS COTTAGE

PSYCHIC SURVEYS
BOOK FIVE:
DESCENSION

PSYCHIC SURVEYS
BOOK SIX:
LEGION

PSYCHIC SURVEYS
BOOK SEVEN:
RISE TO ME

PSYCHIC SURVEYS
BOOK EIGHT:
THE WEIGHT OF THE SOUL

BLAKEMORT
(A PSYCHIC SURVEYS
COMPANION NOVEL
BOOK ONE)

THIRTEEN
(A PSYCHIC SURVEYS
COMPANION NOVEL
BOOK TWO)

ROSAMUND
(A PSYCHIC SURVEYS
COMPANION NOVEL
BOOK THREE)

THIS HAUNTED WORLD
BOOK ONE:
THE VENETIAN

THIS HAUNTED WORLD
BOOK TWO:
THE ELEVENTH FLOOR

THIS HAUNTED WORLD
BOOK THREE:
HIGHGATE

THE JESSAMINE SERIES
BOOK ONE
JESSAMINE

THE JESSAMINE SERIES
BOOK TWO
COMRAICH

REACH FOR THE DEAD
BOOK ONE:
MANDY

REACH FOR THE DEAD
BOOK TWO:
CADES HOME FARM

CARFAX HOUSE:
A CHRISTMAS GHOST STORY

SUMMER OF GRACE

THE
DAMNED
SEASON

A CHRISTMAS GHOST STORY

SHANI STRUTHERS

Dedication

For Misty, for inspiring only the good.

Acknowledgements

The Damned Season is the fourth Christmas Ghost Story I've written – a set of shorter novels including Eve, Blakemort and Carfax House – all of which explore aspects of the paranormal and question what really defines a haunting. Thanks so much to all those who help with ideas and with first drafts, keeping this great tradition alive, after all, who doesn't love a spooky yuletide yarn? So once again thank you to Rob Struthers, Kate Jane Jones, Lesley Hughes, Louisa Taylor and Sarah Savery for beta reader, to Francesca Tyer for editing, and Gina Dickerson of RoseWolf Design for the cover and formatting. Thanks also to you, the reader. Damned season or not, Happy Christmas!

Prologue

SHE'S GONE. VANISHED. Headed outside possibly, where it's dark and cold and lonely. Lonely? That hardly describes it! It's isolated, cut off, removed. A trap! One I willingly walked into. The invitation... The wording on it... I should have ripped it up and thrown it into the bin, set fire to it even, watched as flames caught hold of one corner, hesitant at first, then gaining confidence, becoming lascivious, consuming the entire thing.

But I didn't. I accepted. And now this...

She can't have gone far. This tiny island we've found ourselves on only takes an hour or two to explore. If she went to the boathouse there's no way she'd try to negotiate the sea by herself to reach the mainland. She didn't look like a sailor, didn't look like much of anything to be honest, just scared all the time, from the moment I met her. And now I'm scared too. The things that keep happening here... They're beyond comprehension.

"Crissy!" I shout, and the wind snatches at my voice, devours it.

I'm the only one looking for her. Not them, not the others. They refused, stayed together in the living room, huddled, three of them at least, staring at me when I burst in there and said we had to find her, when I tried to insist. Just…staring. The fourth one, our elusive host, God knows where he went. He keeps disappearing too.

It's so hard to see out here; the night has so much density to it. I'm shaking and my teeth are chattering. It's winter. Deepest winter. Off the coast of northern Wales. Something different, that's what was promised on the invitation. A Christmas to remember. The alternative being to spend it on my own. Again. If only I had.

"CRISSY!"

No matter what's gone on, she shouldn't have run off like that. It may be dangerous in the house, but it's dangerous in the open too. Not an island, not really, not what I was stupid enough to have imagined – somewhere green and lush, a haven. It's little more than a barren rock, the clifftops crumbling away, losing their fight against a vicious sea, waves eating away at them, their intent to destroy. A bad intent or nature striving to eradicate what's unnatural? To erase it from the face of the earth.

I should have brought a torch with me. My eyes simply won't adjust. What if I should wander towards one of those clifftops and be eradicated too?

I blink furiously, but it doesn't help that there are tears in my eyes, also blinding me. I've only known Crissy for a couple of days. I owe her nothing. I could stumble back to the house and console myself that I at least tried to find her. She could be back at the house. But for one thing…that look on her face as she fled. She hasn't gone back. I can feel it in my bones. She wouldn't. That house was destroying her.

"Where the hell are you?"

Mobiles won't work here. They barely worked on the

approach here. So fucking isolated! Once we'd parked, on a strip of land facing the shore, or been dropped off via taxi, we'd had to take a small sailboat across the Irish Sea to reach here. A short burst of a journey, but it'd left me feeling sick. Choppy waves, green not blue, the foam riding on top of them something sickly too. Crissy had also suffered on the ride over. My complexion had matched the sea. Hers, though, had been paler than snow, her eyes fixed solely on the island ahead, never leaving it. Teeth gnawing at her lip the closer we got.

She was different to the other guests, to Tommy, Mel and Drew. Those three were excited to reach the island, congratulating themselves on having escaped 'wretched family duties' as they described them, jokes abounding about not having to wear cringy Christmas jumpers, those knitted by Granny, perhaps, or feeling obliged to attend midnight mass, or sighing at receiving yet more socks as presents. Ironically, some of the things I missed about Christmas. That would never be mine again. They'd been so full of excitement, but smug too, taking their good luck, their families, for granted. Arrogant, I'd go as far as to say. Like I didn't know Crissy, I didn't know them. They didn't know each other either, not until we'd gathered on the boat. Strangers. Our common link, the host. I didn't like them and I was busy telling myself off about that, for being so sure I wouldn't, when the boat finally docked. The man who'd brought us over – of medium height and stocky build, wearing a heavy-duty raincoat with the hood pulled up – jumped onto the jetty, which had a boathouse attached, secured our transport with a rope to a post, then thrust a hand at us. Not a word was said as he helped us off the boat. He hadn't said a word on the journey over either. Still, the three were braying, pointing and giggling.

"There's the house! Look, it's like something out of a Hammer horror movie!"

It wasn't, though, it was rather beautiful, but tired, having to repeatedly endure the beatings that the weather gave it. Victorian and gabled, a turreted room at one corner. Grey brick, blackened in places, and windows like eyes constantly on patrol.

I glanced at Crissy again. No colour had returned to her cheeks.

We'd landed here two days ago, three days before Christmas Day, and we would leave on the 26th. Today was Christmas Eve, early evening, and it had all gone so wrong, had continued to deteriorate after we had set foot on the jetty, the boatman lifting his hand and pointing to the house, opening his mouth finally to utter scant words.

"Go," he'd said. "Go on. Go."

And we did, all five of us, arrogance in the other three diminishing just a little, I noticed, replaced by a tickle of unease. *What is this? What have we got ourselves into?*

Trapped. Like I said. The boatman disappearing as Crissy had disappeared. But he had to be somewhere on the island, didn't he? Like Crissy had to be.

The boathouse was where I'd go now. No other choice really as there's nothing else here, just scrub and bracken, patchy grass and mud. No trees to shelter beneath.

If I turn back to the house, skirt around it, to the front, I can negotiate my way down to the shore. I glance upwards. Ah, the cagey moon, hiding behind clouds, and those clouds growing blacker, a rumble of something that overrides the screaming sea. Thunder?

As scared as I was, it was possible to feel yet more fear. A

4

storm could mean being stranded *beyond* the 26th… No! No! No! If I can find Crissy, if she's all right, then that would be something positive. And we'll leave tomorrow, despite it being Christmas Day, despite the weather too. I was no sailor either, but boatman or no boatman, we'd get away.

"Aargh!"

What was that? Something brushed my face. Feather-light and cold. A bat? It had to be. I whirl around and try to see, once more cursing my useless eyes. Whatever it was has gone. Thank God. A bird would be cold too, wouldn't it? Out here. Just like I am. But why would its touch linger, making me shiver harder than before? I lift my hands again and bring them to my temples, rubbing at the skin there, my teeth still clashing.

Crissy, where are you?

I start to run, not caring that I can barely see, not anymore. I have a plan – to reach the boathouse, and I'll get there by instinct if not by sight alone.

More thunder in the air, teasing me. Like the invitation had teased…

This is definitely the right way. I just have to keep the house to the left of me, a big, dark hulking structure in the corner of my eye. Not really that beautiful at all, but something that squatted in the dark, which lay in wait, smugger even than those inside. It knew you couldn't escape it, no matter how much you wanted to, or how hard you tried.

The roar of the sea grows louder, as if caught in the midst of hysteria. We should never have come here in winter when the weather could turn so quickly. And yet, if there's a defence to be had, it's that we'd been experiencing a mild winter to date, on the mainland at least. Not here, though. Here, the weather is its own entity entirely.

Another structure looms in the dark: the boathouse! There it is. I am going to reach it intact, find Crissy and reassure her, tell her we are leaving, going home.

Home – no matter how bleak, no matter how lonely too – is like a beacon in my mind, spurring me on. Two days I've been here. *Only* two days. Two more to go.

"No!" I put my entire might behind that word; scream it out on the tide of a deep breath. *You will not have me for two more days! Nor any of us.*

Flying on and on, down the hill, arms wheeling, sheer bloody-mindedness the only thing keeping me upright. I won't fall, won't take a tumble. I'll save us.

"Crissy! Crissy! It's all right. I'm here."

What had she seen? Just before she'd fled. What had revealed itself?

You don't have to know!

Not if we were leaving, as soon as the night ended, as dawn broke.

The boathouse. I reach it at last.

Not bricks and mortar but wooden, old and creaky, with a tall, peaked roof. At the door, I push hard. It rattles, but resists, possessive of its quarry.

"Crissy!" I yell again, my throat sore because of the effort. "I'm here! I'm coming in."

Both hands now on the door, I push and pull, push and pull… Is it locked? It can't be. Not if she's in there. If only I was stronger! I throw my entire body weight at it, the impact from my shoulder sending shockwaves through me. I ignore the pain, and the thought of the bruises that will develop. "For God's sake, open, will you?"

Finally, it does.

I practically fall inside. There is no let-up in the darkness, it's just as deep.

This is the boathouse, where the boatman would have secured our transport once we'd disembarked. It'll be here, that boat, bobbing up and down. If only my eyes would adjust!

I hunker down, wary of falling off the ledge, and push my hands out again to feel for the boat. There's nothing, absolutely nothing, and I'm toppling…

Quickly, I straighten up, craning my neck forwards, peering harder into the gloom.

There's no boat. So where is it? Had the boatman simply turned around and left us? Is that why we'd seen nothing of him since? Nothing of anyone. Just us. Just the host… Stranded.

I shake my head, swear. I can't keep thinking about being stranded, can't *deal* with it.

I have to focus on the problem in hand.

"Crissy, are you here? Speak to me. Come on, Crissy, please."

Why I'm whispering, I have no idea. She won't hear me if I whisper.

Even so, I can't bring myself to raise my voice.

The atmosphere in the boathouse, the *empty* boathouse, seems reverent somehow. A strange word to spring to mind, and no idea why it should.

"Crissy?"

That reverence shatters.

There comes a sound like the crack of a whip. Sudden. Sickening.

A flash of white, too. The dress Crissy likes to wear, a

sweatshirt over the top of it.

"CRISSY!"

For the umpteenth time, I yell her name, but there's no hope in it, not anymore.

She's finally revealed herself. She's in front of me. *Swinging*, in front of me.

Her legs, her entire body, jerking so violently.

The boathouse isn't empty after all.

Chapter One

A few days before…

THE DAY STARTED off as ordinary as any other. My name is Beth Williams and I'm twenty-six years old. I live in Edgbaston, Birmingham. It's a nice area, perhaps not quite the best, that would be Digbeth and Erdington, but good enough. It was important to me to live somewhere decent, and to hell with it if the only flat I could afford was the size of a shoebox. I wanted to surround myself with people better than me, people who I could emulate and aspire to. I'm easily influenced. That's what's been said. Prone to trouble…

That was before, however. This is now. My life in London, the place where I grew up, is just a distant memory. I have a job too. One I worked hard at, putting to good use secretarial and administrative skills I'd previously acquired in a quiet office a couple of bus rides away. That's where I was headed that morning, to the office. I'd be early, like I usually was, and I would type and file for eight or so hours before catching two buses home again. Once home, I would shower, cook dinner, and watch a film before bed. That was the routine, five days a week. At weekends, work was replaced with walks, sun-drenched or rain-soaked, my head down, and hands stuffed in pockets, trudging for miles, sometimes admiring the scenery, sometimes ignoring it. Month after month after month. A predictable life. A life I'd chosen. Different from before. It had to be.

It was a Tuesday in mid-December and I was awake even earlier than usual. I was at the small round table in my living room, big enough for two at a pinch, nursing a coffee and staring out the window at raindrops that splattered against the glass. Such a grey day, one I'd have to tackle soon. But not yet. Now was my time to just sit and stare, not checking social media: Facebook, Twitter or Instagram. I deleted those accounts long ago. Nor checking the news on my mobile either. Why depress myself further?

Eventually, I rose from the table, padded the few steps across laminate flooring that showed signs of buckling in several places, to the bathroom to prepare myself.

Twenty-six. Sometimes I thought I looked older than that, sometimes far younger. Today, though, it was like I carried the weight of the world on my shoulders. Blue eyes held no sparkle; brown hair was limp and the skin on my cheeks sallow. I wasn't ugly, I wasn't pretty, but somewhere in between. I didn't gaze at myself for too long. I never did. Just performed the necessary functions before heading to the bedroom to exchange nightclothes for a skirt, blouse, and jacket. I'd tie my hair back too in a ponytail, and wear flat shoes and tights, the aim to look as neat and efficient as possible. To blend in.

It was almost time to leave and walk the ten minutes to the first bus stop, only a quick sandwich to make beforehand. Ham or cheese was my favourite, pickle on either. I'd also stuff a bag of crisps into my bag, salt and vinegar, and a chocolate bar. Not overly healthy, but not too bad. Just an average lunch, that would be eaten at my desk or on a bench a few yards from the office, a small insurance firm, with only the pigeons for company.

Ready now, I made my way to the front door, down the shortest, the narrowest of hallways, one I'd tried to brighten with simple white paint. There was something on the mat, causing me to frown. An envelope. At this hour? Usually, the post didn't arrive till much later. A simple square envelope, whiter than the walls – it was pristine.

My hands shook for some reason as I bent to retrieve it. Of course I received post, bills and circulars mainly, but not something like this. Just by glancing at it, I could tell this was more personal. I turned it over. There was my name – and address – penned in ink, the letters with a flair to them, especially the 'B' of Beth and 'W' of Williams. Who had written to me? Moreover, how had they got this address? I'd shared it with hardly anyone. There were ways, I supposed, for the persistent. So who had done exactly that and persisted?

I could have solved the mystery there and then, opened that starched envelope and cast it aside, revealed its contents. But if I didn't get moving, I'd miss my bus, I'd be late. My track record tarnished. Hesitating still, but only for a few more seconds, I placed the envelope in my bag, in an interior pocket and finally left my flat, head down, as usual, and hurried along damp streets, reaching the bus stop with only a minute to spare.

The bus at this hour wasn't too busy, not like the later ones, which was why I preferred it, I could always get a seat. Twenty minutes on this one, then twenty on the next, and

I'd reach my destination. Time to stare out of windows again, to contemplate…

Christmas was coming, so many houses with trees in their windows, although the lights that adorned them wouldn't twinkle until the return journey home. Some of the more enthusiastic residents had decorated the outside of their houses too, with an assortment of Santa's, reindeers and snowmen, the usual offenders. There was no escaping the season, it was everywhere I looked. Shops having gone all out too, a few of them anyway.

My stomach clenched. I'd lived in Birmingham for a few years now; this would be…what? My fourth or fifth Christmas spent here? As usual, I was dreading it. The loneliness that I otherwise tolerated, nurtured even, beginning to ache. I'd have been happy to keep working over the holiday, but my firm was shutting down for it, my bosses adopting benevolent smiles when they'd announced, yet again, they'd be observing this tradition.

"I'm sure you're all looking forward to some time off, and some of you will be travelling, no doubt, or wanting to spend time with families. I expect you're all very excited."

Everyone had smiled back, nodded. But me? I'd shrivelled inside. My *soul* had shrivelled. How patronising Mark Cornell, one of the partners, sounded! How dare he tar everyone with the same brush! Not everyone had family, or plans, or friends. Why assume? Why switch off the life-support machine?

I was shaking again, on the No.49 heading east. Getting angry. I mustn't. I knew that. Had to get myself under control. Take deep, gentle breaths, in for a count of four, out for a count of four. Focus on something positive in my mind, a place that I liked, somewhere far from the city, deep in the countryside, surrounded by buttercup meadows, perhaps, or with a view of the sea. I just had to close my eyes and drift, wait for the anger to burn itself out.

The envelope in my bag. That was the image that appeared in my mind. Anger indeed dissolving but replaced with a curiosity that burnt just as much.

I'd always been curious, always wanted to know everything. Ironic, really, when all I wanted now was to forget.

But I couldn't forget the envelope.

Quick enough, the first bus journey was over. I disembarked, rushed along to another bus stop, and waited there. A few minutes later, the No.60 arrived, busier than the 49, but I found a seat in one of the middle rows. A window seat too – more Christmas trees in houses to look at, more shop windows plastered with fake snow. How grubby that would look post-Christmas, turning grey and patchy in places. Taking weeks for someone to scrub it off, the greasy stain of it lasting well into spring.

The envelope… What was the purpose of it?

For God's sake, Beth, there's only one way to find out. Open it!

Although there was no one beside me, there were people in front and at the back. What if whoever was at the back peered over my shoulder and started to read it too? That would annoy me, make me angry again. This – whatever 'this' was – was for my eyes only. If I shifted my body, though, and almost huddled into the window, that would make it difficult for them to do so. Then I could see what it contained, read it in peace.

The bus shuddered to a halt. More people got on. I rolled my eyes. One of them, a middle-aged man, rotund, with reddened cheeks, was wearing bright red reindeer antlers. Why did people do that, wantonly make fools of themselves and all in the name of Christmas? Such an inane grin on his face, as if he'd already been nipping at the sherry.

My heart sank further. He was coming towards me, his eyes fixated on my face, such glee in them, like I was a long-lost friend instead of a stranger.

"D'ya mind, love?" he said.

Without waiting for an answer, he sat down beside me, his bulk forcing me to huddle against the window after all. Now was not the time to dig out the envelope, especially as he was trying to engage me in further conversation.

"On your way to work?"

"Yes," I replied, keeping my gaze averted.

"It's a treadmill, eh?"

I nodded. For some maybe, but not for me, no matter how mundane my duties.

"Still," he continued, "this'll give 'em a laugh." He gestured upwards, as if the antlers were something that needed to be pointed out, as if I hadn't seen them.

When I remained silent, he carried on regardless. "Looking forward to it?"

"To what?" I said, and then cursed my stupidity. I knew what he meant; I didn't need him to elaborate. I should have said 'yes' again and left it at that.

My two-word response had indeed encouraged him. "To Christmas, of course!" he boomed. "Bit of fun, isn't it? They say it's just for the kids, but I disagree. It's for everyone. A chance to let your hair down and enjoy yourself. Any excuse, though, eh?"

Rip-roaring laughter escaped him, a blast that made the seat judder as much as the bus. "Talking of enjoying yourself," he continued, "I'm looking forward to the works do. That's always a riot! I expect you are too, getting dressed up and slapping on a bit of make-up."

He meant well. I kept telling myself that, but mentally I was pleading for him to stop, to leave me alone. Yes, there'd be a 'works do', drinks and lunch at our local pub, all staff invited, all expected to turn up, benevolent smiles on the bosses' faces yet again, because they were picking up the tab, *treating* us. Everyone would be bolting their food, though, draining their drinks, going through the motions because they were just so eager to get away – to join *real* friends. I was wondering if I could cry off the whole event, say I had a cold or something at the last minute. Hardly anyone talked to me anyway.

This man was talking, though, had just bumped his shoulder against mine. "Oh, they're a dour lot on this bus, aren't they?" he said, too loudly. "No one would ever know it's almost Christmas. Shall we liven them up, sing a song or something?"

He opened his mouth wider, began to massacre Live Aid's 'Do They Know it's Christmas', nudging me again, telling me to join in.

"Sorry," I said. "This is my stop. Do you mind?"

This time it was me who didn't give him a chance to reply as I stood up, as red as the antlers, and barged my way past him. If he said something to me, maybe apologised or, more likely, comment on how uptight I was, I didn't hear it. I flew down that aisle, off the bus and onto the street, nowhere near my work, a good fifteen minutes' walk still to go.

The rain continued to fall as I half ran, half walked, my hood pulled up, but still I was getting soaked. I'd arrive at work a sodden, harried mess, to sit there all day in damp clothing, the radio turned on, albeit low, and pumping out the same rotating Christmas tunes, the DJs cramming them all in whilst they could, hour after hour.

Out of breath, I had to stop. Despite having got off the bus much earlier than usual, being *forced* to, I still wouldn't be late. No need to panic. Time was on my side, enabling me to stop in a doorway, perhaps, to satisfy a curiosity that was only mounting.

I did just that. And to hell with the fact that the window of the shop whose doorway I'd chosen to shelter in was festooned with tinsel. I couldn't go a minute longer wondering what I was carrying in my bag. It felt…momentous, somehow. Vital.

I'd envisaged opening the envelope carefully, rather than tearing into it, but the latter is exactly what I did, hands just too eager. And there it was, not a letter, but an invitation, one with the most peculiar heading.

The Damned Season. *You are invited to join me at my island home December 22nd- 26th off the coast of Anglesey, for Christmas with a difference. Directions and timings on the back of the invite. You'll be met at Hinch Point for the short journey by boat to the island. All drinks and food provided. Looking forward to seeing you. Peter.*

At first, all I could do was stare at it, at more beautifully handwritten words. I was being invited somewhere for Christmas, by a man I was struggling to remember. Peter? Peter who? I *had* known a Peter, hadn't I? A long time ago. Could it be him?

Peter… Peter Bexan. That was the man, or rather boy, I'd known. God, it really was years ago. I hadn't thought about him in ages. And yet he'd thought about me…

Everything around me faded as I continued to stare at the invitation.

A chance. An opportunity. An island. Somewhere green and peaceful, like the place I'd imagine in my head when I needed to relax, to breathe easier.

I couldn't go, could I? Just take off like that?

Was I the only one invited, or would there be more? I was appalled and relieved by both prospects. Why relieved, though? Why appalled? Of course I wouldn't go! It'd cost money to get to Hinch Point – the meeting point that was detailed on the back – a train ride, and then a taxi no doubt. Money that I needed. But to spend on what? Not presents, I had no one to buy for. Not on food or drink either, not if it was provided.

I shook my head, raindrops flying in different directions as the lights inside the shop window came on, reflecting against the tinsel in a garish manner. An assistant appeared in the window, adding yet more festive tat to an already groaning display. A woman who saw me hunched there and smiled at me, a smile that said 'isn't this fun? Don't you just love Christmas!' Another one who assumed.

Just like Peter assumed. *Looking forward to seeing you.*

I studied the invite again. There was no RSVP. He didn't just assume I was coming. It was like he knew.

Christmas with a difference. How different? Perhaps we wouldn't celebrate at all. Perhaps the difference was that there'd be no Christmas. Just splendid isolation.

The Damned Season. What a peculiar way to put it.

As Christmas jingles blared from the shop, my lip curled. What an *apt* way.

Chapter Two

PETER BEXAN... COME to think of it, there had been a slight lilt to his voice, a twang of some sort creeping through. The clue was in his surname, I suppose. Bexan was a Welsh name, although I only realised this after I'd googled it, googled *him*. Nothing about him on the net, though. I'd even created Facebook and Twitter accounts to try to find him, but there was no one that fitted the bill that I recognised. I was around...sixteen, seventeen when I knew him, I think? It's all a bit blurred to be honest. He was different to the usual set of people I hung around with. Quieter, more self-effacing, and not a school friend. He was a couple of years older than me, perhaps three or four.

I'd arrived at the office, the first as usual, but only by a hair's breadth this time. I had switched on the lights, hung up my wet coat, and then set about making a fresh pot of coffee for everyone. I loved the aroma of coffee, wondered if anyone else did too as they entered the office first thing – it was such a welcoming smell. If they did, they never said, never commented, 'Oh great, you've got the coffee on, *again*. Thank you. Could really do with a cup.' Instead, they'd shrug their coats off, just as I had, grab themselves a mug and absentmindedly fill it to the brim before taking it to their respective desks. As if it was the coffee fairies responsible for having made it, for keeping them topped up with caffeine throughout the day. *Don't expect thanks.* I didn't but…just once in a while it'd be nice. It wasn't part of my job description, but someone had to do it, as well as wash the mugs at the end of the day, the filter pot too, and stow them neatly away in the cupboards.

As I sipped my coffee, I sighed. I had a mountain of work to sort through that day, couldn't keep trawling through the social network sites, letter after letter to type, and reports as well. There were also claims that needed filing. I looked up, towards a small room in which older paperwork was kept. The whole system needed computerising as far as I was concerned, to be brought into the twenty-first century. It was haphazard in there, stuff put in wrong date or name order. I just never had enough time to rectify the situation, always too busy dealing with newer claims. If I could come in over Christmas, though, that would be an ideal time to sort it. I wondered if I should raise the possibility with my bosses; I wouldn't need paying, I'd tell them. I could take a day or two off in lieu. That was how desperate I was to fill those dead days. Or…there was another option. One that had only recently presented itself. I could travel for Christmas; visit a blast from the past.

Although I was at my computer, although my hands were on the keyboard, tap, tap, tapping away, although – inevitably – someone had turned on the radio, George Michael crooning 'Last Christmas', my mind continued to wander, to debate, to *rationalise*.

Peter had worked behind the counter of a convenience store I used to pop into, one of those that proudly declared they were open from the crack of dawn till late. Not a busy shop, sometimes I was the only one in there, and we'd get talking, the pair of us, just passing the time of day. It was me who did much of the talking, actually. He was shy at first. Had a strange smile too. There always seemed to be an apology in it. That was what drew me to him, not because I fancied him or anything, it was because he was different.

"D'ya like working in here?" I'd asked.

"S'okay," he'd answered.

"It's quiet, I suppose. You get to do your own thing."

His face had brightened. "Yeah. Yeah, there is that."

"Do you live locally too?"

"For now."

"Can I…um…have a packet of Marlborough, please? A ten-pack."

"Cigarettes?"

"Yeah."

"You're too young to buy cigarettes."

Of course I was, just sixteen, but still I'd persisted. "Please. No one's watching."

His smile was sympathetic. "More than my job's worth."

I'd smiled too, and then shrugged. "Whatever. I'll just take this, then." I'd grabbed a bar of chocolate instead, reached into my pocket before deciding to have a bit more fun.

"It's not just money I've got in my pocket, you know."

He'd raised an eyebrow. "Oh?"

"Nope. I've got something else, something…lethal."

A frown had developed, but he didn't say anything, didn't avert his eyes either.

"A knife," I'd elaborated. "Now give me the ciggies, or else."

Our gaze had held, as if we were transfixed. No fear in

20

his eyes, no surprise either. It was as if he'd *expected* this.

I'd burst out laughing. "Hey! I'm only kidding." I'd been embarrassed actually, that I'd been so dumb, so childish, trying to spice things up a little.

He was gracious, though, and laughed along with me. "Good. I'm relieved. Still no ciggies, though, knife or no knife."

"The chocolate will do," I'd assured him, handing over the money and waiting for change. That stunt, pathetic though it was, was what had broken the ice between us and from thereon in, we'd chat regularly, I'd look forward to it, making excuses to pop into the shop more and more often. Then I stopped calling…because of the accident. After that, everything changed. But before then, it had just been so easy between us.

He *was* a friend. A good friend. Not that we ever met outside the shop, roamed the streets, hung out in the park, or visited the cinema, and never was there a suggestion of a romance between us. The only place we were together was in the convenience shop, sometimes for half an hour or more, sometimes every single day. I'd enter his world, and we'd…talk. About shit mostly. Stupid stuff. I even helped him stack shelves occasionally.

"Keeps you out of trouble," he'd joke.

If only.

We just got on, Peter and me. We were relaxed in each other's company. He rented a room in a house about thirty minutes' walk from the shop. And…it's coming back to me now…he said he liked living in London, the hustle and bustle of it, the excitement, but that he wouldn't stay indefinitely, because there was a house, a family house, and one day he'd inherit it. A house that was far, far away…

Funny I hadn't recalled this in so long, and yet the information was all there, stored in my brain, coming to the fore when summoned. He'd said he was getting his fix of life now, that's *exactly* how he put it, because at this house he was due to inherit, there wasn't much life. Or rather, there was none. It was isolated. On an island, the only one on it. A house that faced the main shore, glowered back at it, that sat and brooded.

Peter may have worked in a store, but he was pretty erudite. He knew words and how to use them to embellish what he was saying. He impressed me with his language, made me imagine that house so vividly, and how alone it was.

"What will you do for money, though?" I'd said, so curious. "How can you afford to live in a house on an island, in the middle of nowhere?"

He hadn't looked particularly fazed. "That's why I'm working hard now, I suppose. So that I *will* have enough." It was almost closing time, not another soul around, and so we'd grabbed a couple of cokes from the chiller and were standing around, like we always did, chatting. "It's a dream, though, isn't it, to have a house like that?"

"Never been my dream," I said, taking a slurp of coke.

"You sure about that?"

What a strange thing to ask! Of course I was sure!

"It's just…" he continued, "…everyone dreams of getting away sometimes."

"Maybe, but to a house on an island?"

"To a house on an island in Wales," he elaborated wryly. Sighing, he added, "I suppose I've always known I'd inherit the house. I just accepted it."

I may have deemed myself curious, but only now I was

22

asking more questions in my mind. *What if you'd refused? What if you'd decided you preferred life in London? What if you'd met someone and had kids, would you drag them out there too?*

He hadn't refused, though, and as for being married, the invite was from him…just him.

I was flattered by it, I had to admit. No one had wanted me for so long. Not even my parents, whom I was estranged from.

My fingers ached from all the typing I was doing; my brain ached too, dredging up so many memories, remembering suddenly something that had seemed insignificant, compared to so much else, anyway. I had to give myself a break, fetch a drink.

Rising from my chair, I walked to the relaxation suite, a glorified name for a cubbyhole, with kitchen units, a sink, a plastic table and chairs. Some people were at their desks, working diligently away, those that weren't, two of them, were in the cubbyhole. I could hear their voices as I approached, my steps slowing.

"What are you going to wear to the Christmas party?" said one, Caroline.

"God, nothing special. Why? Are you?" replied Lorraine, Caroline's sidekick.

"No, I suppose not. Wish we were having a real party, you know, an evening meal at a fancy hotel and a club afterwards, not just lunch at a pub. I'd dress up then!"

"If you dress up, Mark'd notice you."

"Lorraine, he's married!"

"So?"

A burst of laughter. "You are *bad*!"

"But you love me anyway."

"Yeah, I do," admitted Caroline, who, like Lorraine, was somewhere in her late twenties. "I'd be bored out of my mind here if I didn't have you."

"Ah, you'd survive! You could always pal up with…" There was a brief silence as I continued to eavesdrop, wanting that coffee, but feeling it too rude to burst in on them. Again, curiosity kicked in. Who could Caroline pal up with?

"Don't say it," Caroline cut through the silence. "Not her."

Her?

"She's odd, though, isn't she?"

"*Really* odd."

"Keeps herself to herself."

"Thank God."

"Always so eager to please."

"You know why, don't you?"

"Well…kinda. Can't be true, though. Can it?"

"I don't know. But at the Christmas party we could have some fun with her, get her drunk, make her spill the beans. You know what? I'm looking forward to it after all!"

I stepped back. No matter how thirsty I was, no way I was going in there now. No names had been mentioned, it *could* be a coincidence, I wasn't the only one who kept myself to myself at the office, Eva and Jenny did too. They just came in, did their job and went home, were polite to everyone, but that was about it. This so-called rumour could concern one of them. Were they eager to please? As eager as I was? *To toe the line.* That I didn't know. What if it *was* me they meant, and they knew about my past, not just our guiding lights, the directors, who had to be told when I came for the interview – the accident had caused a bit of a stir

24

when it had happened, it had made the nationals. If they'd googled my name, found out what was attached to it…well, it was best to explain. Somehow, though, Caroline and Lorraine had found out too, done a little digging of their own, or overheard something. What if the latter were true, what if my bosses had been talking about me for whatever reason, their heads together, eyes wide and gossiping, like old women at the gallows rather than our hallowed superiors? And Caroline had caught snatches of it, as had Lorraine, both now intent on grilling me. *Exposing* me.

My cheeks were burning as I returned to my seat. If it was me they meant, if they knew, something of it at least, then soon the whole office would. And then they'd look at me the way people have always looked at me since, with disgust, with no understanding at all. At my desk, I had to force myself to breathe evenly again, try to calm the beating of my erratic heart. Would my past always haunt me? I'd changed! I had! The move to Birmingham, my job, all proved it. I just wanted to be normal again, a regular girl. Like Caroline, like Lorraine, Eva and Jenny. Nothing sordid about me.

Although my sight was blurred with tears, I saw well enough as Caroline and Lorraine sashayed past my desk, back to their own. Clocked how they both glanced my way, certain that Caroline had nudged Lorraine, the pair of them trying to stifle giggles.

My hands, placed on my desk, bunched into fists. In that moment, despite a burst of laughter from somewhere else in the office, light laughter, and the cheerful Christmas jingle that was currently playing, I felt I could leap over my desk, rush up to the sniggering pair and strangle them with my bare hands, murder them. And this time…this time I'd enjoy the experience. I'd savour how shock would turn to fear, to desperation, to pleading and sorrow. I'd ignore that pleading. My grip growing tighter…

Stop! Enough! Don't let them get to you. Everybody deserves a second chance!

I deserved a second chance. Didn't I?

Worse than the anger were the doubts, and how quickly they crept in.

I had to get out of there, take an early break, dreading the walk to the door, not sure my legs would carry me. Nonetheless, I grabbed my bag, hauled myself to my feet, and with head low, rushed from the office, leaving my coat behind but not caring, unable to breathe properly, needing fresh, sweet air to fill my lungs. Onwards I continued, to the park bench, where even now the pigeons sat expectantly. I slumped down on it, trying desperately to keep howls of despair at bay. There was no escape. Everything I'd built, the new life I'd forged, was so fragile. Because of choices I'd made. Because of a mistake!

My bag wasn't the only thing I'd grabbed on the way out. I'd grabbed the invitation too, was now clutching it to my chest as more memories emerged, what Peter had said about this house I'd been invited to.

"I'm not like you," he'd said, "I don't hate people."

"I don't hate people!" I'd protested.

"There's an anger in you, though."

"There isn't—"

"A restlessness."

Again I'd tried to protest. Again he'd spoken over me.

"I don't hate people, but they can be a pain." He'd then grinned. "Present company excepted."

"I should bloody hope so," I'd retorted, also with a grin.

"Thing is, I don't want to be surrounded by concrete all my life, I like the countryside, open spaces. I like the tranquillity of it."

"Yeah, yeah," I'd agreed, thinking how nice he was making it sound.

"When I've got my house, on my island, you'll have to visit."

"Maybe." No matter how nice, I couldn't imagine it. Had other things on my mind.

I could imagine it now, though. Being away from Birmingham, the office, and the people in it. The Christmas party was on the 22nd, and then we were closed until the New Year. If I *was* going to the island, I'd be travelling on the 22nd and therefore have a bona fide excuse to avoid it.

I recalled Caroline's words. *We could have some fun with her, get her drunk, make her spill the beans.* If it was me they meant, I could also spoil their fun. With no witch-hunt to occupy them, the Christmas party would be every bit as boring as it normally was.

I lowered my hands and looked at the invitation again. *The Damned Season.* It'd been years since I'd seen Peter, since he'd offered me his friendship. And here he was again, offering me something else, a haven, somewhere to run to. If there were other people going, it didn't matter, they'd be strangers, they'd know nothing about me. I could do what I did here and keep myself to myself, spend time exploring the island, clear my head, plan my next move even. Because again, if it was me Caroline and Lorraine had been referring to, I couldn't stay, I'd be the centre of attention whilst being shunned further.

Just a few days away, with an old friend, no meal for one on Christmas Day, and, fingers crossed, no Queen's speech.

Christmas with a difference. I'd take this opportunity, which right now seemed like my own Christmas miracle. I'd swagger back into the office, let it be known I'd be finishing work on the evening of the 21st, *because I had plans.*

Thank you, Peter, I whispered, feeling so much calmer now.

Chapter Three

IT HAD TAKEN me nearly four hours to reach Hinch Point, having taken a train from Birmingham's New Street Station all the way to Anglesey, itself another island, connected to the rest of Wales by a suspension bridge, and then a taxi from Holyhead further round the coast. A gruelling journey. On the train, people had occupied all seats and were standing in the aisles too, some of them weary-looking, others bright-eyed, chatting to those standing beside them, telling them they were travelling home for Christmas.

I suppose, because I had somewhere to go too, I didn't begrudge them too much, not this time. I felt included. Not so much of an outsider. We thundered our way past scenery that would look lush in summer but tended towards bleak in winter, vivid greens having given way to more bruised shades of the spectrum. Leaning my head against the window, relishing the coolness of it, as the carriage was clammy from the heat of so many bodies, I thought back to when I'd told my bosses I wouldn't be around for the Christmas party. Eyebrows had risen, surprise hastily concealed. *You've got friends? Who'd have thought it?* Perhaps I was being paranoid thinking that, paranoid too thinking I was the person Caroline and Lorraine had been talking about. God knows they hadn't bothered to look my way again, not even when I'd let Lorraine know I was going to be away for Christmas, when she'd been in the kitchen with me, grabbing a coffee from the pot I'd just brewed.

"Oh," she'd said. "Really?"

"Yes, I'm going to stay with a friend."

"Nice," was her only other comment as she drifted off.

Paranoia gripped me even now. Had I read it all wrong? Did I *always* read it wrong? Ever since the accident. Was paranoia now something inherent in me? I straightened up, forsook the coolness of the window and bit my lip instead, trying not to surrender to self-pity, at least. In recent years I'd seen a counsellor, just a few sessions. I couldn't afford more. "The past is the past," the counsellor told me. "All that exists is the present." I shouldn't think too much about the future. Just take life one step at a time, get through it, treading as lightly as I could. And to breathe deep, breathe evenly, impossible to panic then, to spiral ever downwards. Instead of focussing on myself, I thought about Peter. As I said, there was no RSVP on the invite, and no telephone number either. All he'd said was we'd be met at Hinch Point at 3pm to be ferried across to the island, then returned on the morning of the 26th. Luckily, the trains were running on Boxing Day, I'd already checked, a skeleton service. Then it would all be over, for another year at least. I was looking forward to seeing Peter, to seeing how life had treated him. Was he still the same humble person he was back then, or had being Lord of the Manor changed him? I hoped not. If he was full of himself, then I'd leave the island, come home sooner than the 26th. No one was going to Lord it over me!

Again, I had to tell myself to stop with the paranoia, or

was it more like anger? Peter was a good person, and it was nice of him to invite me, fulfilling an age-old promise. Even if he knew what I'd done. *Especially* if he knew.

Don't dwell! No, I wouldn't. Besides, the journey, as taxing as it was, was flying by. It'd been ages since I'd last been on a train. I should just enjoy it. Try not to think at all...

The train was exchanged for a taxi, and at last I arrived at Hinch Point, the cabby having dropped me off, and waved goodbye, seeming to shoot off at great speed. How incredulous he'd been when I'd told him my destination – the house on the island.

"Anghyfannedd?" he'd said, and in the rear-view mirror I could see how his big, bushy eyebrows had shot up.

"Angher-what?" I'd endeavoured to repeat. "Is that what it's called?"

"It's what we call it round here."

"Never heard that word before."

"You're not Welsh, are you? So why would you?"

"What does it mean?"

"Desolate, love," he'd replied, his voice heavy with the accent of his homeland. "That's what it means. Why on earth anyone would want to live there is beyond me."

He'd driven off just as another car rounded the corner, coming towards me, that car pulling up on the layby I stood in, someone disembarking.

"All right, love?" a man said. "You here for Pete?"

"Pete?" I'd never shortened his name before. "Yes. Yes, I am. You are too?"

"Sure. Thought it might be a laugh. The name's Drew by the way."

The man called Drew stepped closer with his hand

outstretched. I took it whilst quietly assessing him. Fairly tall, he was also dark-haired and dark-eyed with a bit of a goatee beard going on, quite wispy in places. He was about my age too, and rangy in build, wearing tight fitting charcoal trousers, polished shoes with a pointed toe, and a padded jacket. He looked, in my opinion anyway, a bit of a likely lad, someone guilty of selling dodgy watches for a living, but who sold a lot of them. His clothes weren't cheap, and the aftershave he wore, which I kept catching whiffs of, wasn't a cheap smell either, it had the reek of money. Not really the kind of man I'd envisage Peter being friends with at all.

"So how well do you know Peter?" I said, trying to make conversation as we stood there. About to reply, he was distracted, as I was, by another car heading towards us.

"Oh, who's this?" he said. "Looks like we're having a right old party!"

Another man parked up and exited the car, one in the same mould as Drew. He came over and introduced himself – Tommy – and asked if we were waiting to be ferried over to see Peter. I wanted to shake my head at his question, even though that was far from fair. After all, I'd asked the same of Drew. But seriously, what else would we be doing in such a forlorn spot, with the wind blowing and the light beginning to fade?

Another car appeared, and then a taxi. A woman alighted from each. Inwardly, I sighed with relief. I wasn't going to be the only female on the island then.

The woman in the car was Mel, and the woman in the taxi was Crissy. Both barely had time to introduce themselves before Drew started pointing.

"There's the boat, look. Bang on 3pm, like the invite

said. Christ, the ferryman looks like something from the Middle Ages, doesn't he, the way his hood's pulled up like that?"

Although a slight exaggeration, I knew what he meant. The man on the boat, now gliding towards us on a sea that, thankfully, looked relatively calm, wore a dark grey sowester, and as Drew had said, the hood was pulled all the way up. On seeing him, we all moved closer, picking our way over a thin strand of pebble beach that reeked of seaweed to a simple wooden jetty, to wait for him there. I couldn't see his expression or anything of his face really, because of the hood, but the word that sprung to mind if I had to describe him was 'grim'. Unfair, perhaps, but that was the vibe he exuded.

"Here," Tommy's grin was lop-sided. "No one's got any pennies on them, have they?"

"Pennies?" Mel said. She was also grinning widely. "Why?"

"Cos if you have, keep them in your pocket."

Again Mel wanted to know why.

"Haven't you heard the song? You know, that one by Chris de Burgh." Tommy took a deep breath and started to sing. "*Don't pay the ferryman. Don't even fix the price. Don't pay the ferryman. Until he gets you to the other side.*"

Mel and Drew dissolved into fits of laughter on hearing this, Tommy joining them as soon as he'd finished his rendition, actually whooping at one point. I smiled too, more in an effort to join in rather than because I found it funny – something about it *wasn't* funny, it was a little too close for comfort. As for Crissy, she kept her eyes glued to the boat heading our way and refused to smile at all.

Tommy had done it, though, he'd broken the ice,

bonded with Drew and Mel at least, the three of them now chatting away to each other, just random stuff, commenting on the weather, and how we'd found ourselves in the 'arse end of nowhere' as Tommy put it, because that's how desperate we were, all five of us, to escape Christmas, that desperation causing more raucous laughter between them.

These types of exchanges were still going on as the boat docked and we were beckoned – yes, *beckoned* over, by the boatman, with a crook of his finger.

Once on board, I studied my fellow holidaymakers more closely, Mel and Crissy in particular. Mel was pretty, she had reddish hair, auburn I supposed you'd call it, pale freckled skin and pale eyes too, ethereal, but for a hardness that existed in both her voice and her whole demeanour, a determined edge. She wasn't the floaty female she portrayed, but one of the lads. Again, I was surprised that Peter knew people like these. I just…I wouldn't have guessed it. Crissy, though, was different. Younger than me, she had to be, by at least two or three years, she was also pretty, but in a far more discreet way, with brown hair, brown eyes, and skin that looked like the sun had never touched it. Small framed, she was dressed in an overcoat that swamped her. *She* was the kind of person I could imagine Peter knowing, quiet, like him, but there was another side to him clearly, a side that liked people like Drew, Tommy and Mel, more overt people. And he must have really liked them, because he'd invited them here, to this island, for Christmas.

Anghyfannedd. A place of desolation. I don't know why, but I'd barely glanced at the island before now, had somehow kept my eyes averted. But it was only a mile or so off the coast, maybe when the tides went far out, you could even walk to it, just like you could at that place down in

Penzance, St Michael's Mount. Who knew? So really, it was pretty hard to avoid. And yet I'd done exactly that, so much happening otherwise to occupy me.

The boat had set sail, the boatman steering but not saying a word, causing more giggles from the three that had banded together, an unwelcome reminder of Caroline and Lorraine and how, just like them, they tried to stifle their laughter but in a deliberately half-hearted manner. As I eventually raised my eyes, I swallowed, hard. Desolate was right. The island was small, as Peter said it was, something black, volcanic almost, that emerged from the sea, *interrupted* it. *How can he stand to live there?* I couldn't. Right away, I knew that. Thank God it was just a few days I'd have to endure it. *Endure?* I glanced again at the people on the boat, and didn't detract that sentiment.

"There'd better be plenty of food and drink, like the invite says," Drew said.

"Not bothered by the food," Mel chimed in. "Just the drink. I want it on tap, all day, every day." She then turned her attention to the boatman. "Excuse me…um…whatever your name is, this house, it's posh, is it? If the drink runs out, you okay to fetch more?"

He ignored her. Continued to navigate the seas, which were churning more and more, making me feel sick, disorientated, confused even. What had I done coming here? To see a person who might have been a friend once but was now a stranger to me. More to the point, what had he done, inviting these others? They were awful. There and then that's what I decided, the last people I'd want to be stuck with. All friends of Peter, gathered together for Christmas – the only thing we seemingly had in common being that it was a season we disliked, hated even, that we wanted an escape from. But escape here?

I really was feeling very ill, unable to listen to their banter anymore, trying to make like the boatman and ignore it, praying that my room, wherever it was in Peter's house, was far, far away from everyone. Crissy was silent too, and just so pale. A mistake. Perhaps that's what this was. But what was the alternative? For me, at least. I'd have had the Christmas party to contend with otherwise, Caroline and Lorraine, and then…nothing, just my own company, my own thoughts, circling in my head. The company of strangers *was* preferable. As for Peter, soon I'd discover how he had found me, found any of us. The chosen few. That's what it seemed like. Chosen for what?

We docked, thank God. I was seriously about to hurl. Just as we'd been ushered onto the boat, we were now ushered off, the boatman holding out his hand, me not wanting to take it, unnerved by him as I was by this whole experience.

And then he uttered his first, his *only* words. "Go. Go on. Go."

Up to the house.

There it was, in view at last, set back on the island, a steep path leading up to it.

Waiting.

Chapter Four

IT WASN'T AN ugly house, like something out of a 'Hammer horror' as Tommy, Drew and Mel described it. It was a big house, though, I'd give it that. It was odd. More its location than anything else. A proper mansion, set here, on a rock, occupied by whom, just Peter? When really it was a house that should be teeming with life, a family, several kids running wild and free, embracing nature and all the elements. Perhaps he did have a family, I reminded myself, but somehow I didn't think so. The atmosphere the island was drenched in, the day fading in earnest, the sun not so much setting as just winking out, was not one imbued with the laughter and innocence of children. *Innocence.* A strange word to come to mind but one I couldn't shake as I did what the boatman had said and followed Crissy and the others up the path and steps that led to the entrance of the house. It felt lonely here, abandoned even. It felt…guilty of something. Christmas spent here certainly would be different, that was for sure.

The closer we drew to the house, the quieter the others became. Not Crissy, who was quiet anyway, but the other three, not so gung-ho as they were on the boat, so entitled.

I could empathise. Unease sat in the pit of my stomach

too, not helped by the mysterious boatman, who, when I turned to see, was standing on the jetty still, watching us, as if making sure we didn't bolt back down the hill and demand he return us, that we fulfilled our agreement to go inside the house. Well, of course we would! I, for one, had come a long way. A return journey was not on the cards, not tonight, at any rate. I'd give this experience a shot at least. Who knew, I might end up enjoying myself? There might be other guests, but as long as we weren't forced to live in each other's pockets, it'd be okay. The house was big enough to suggest we could have our own space.

Unease. Was that too insipid a word for it? That house, as we continued to climb upwards, *loomed* over us. So many windows, an extraordinary amount, and at the centre of it all, an oak door that sat sulkily within a deep porch. A turret too, probably housing the main bedroom. A mix of styles, really. I'm no architect, but parts of it looked older than mere Victorian. All of it looked weathered, though. It looked defiant. No storm, no matter how intense it got, was going to dislodge it. That house had been built here, on this rock, a house that belonged to Peter's family, handed down through the generations, and here it would stay. Come what may. Was Peter happy here? I looked around, at the starkness of it all, no lawned gardens surrounding the house, just land, and, of course, the sea. Not that far from the mainland, not really, but even so, could anyone be happy with such isolation? Splendid isolation I'd called it, but it didn't seem that way now. As much as I didn't tend to like people, not anymore, as much as it was best to avoid them, I didn't think I could bear it with only the circling gulls for company. The circling gulls… I looked up. There should be seabirds aplenty, squawking around an island like this.

There weren't, though. The sky, deepening by the minute, becoming indigo, was empty.

We'd reached the entrance to the house, the door remaining closed as we gathered round it.

"Jeez, thanks for the warm welcome, Pete."

It was Tommy speaking, trying to sound like a regular cheeky chappy, but there it was, in his voice, the unease I'd guessed he was feeling.

Tommy was around mid to late twenties – the same age bracket as Peter, as the rest of us, blond hair close cropped, eyes like slits and cheeks all doughy. Like Drew, like Mel, he turned my stomach. Maybe I was the one being arrogant. Maybe they were looking at me, at Crissy even, who was trembling, I was sure of it, but then it was cold, it was getting chilly indeed, and thinking the same thing: who'd want to be friends with them? An unlikely quintet, and soon we'd be six.

Peter might not have been waiting for us at the door, arms wide open in greeting, but we had to get inside and get warm. Taking the initiative, I stepped forward and located the knocker, which was fed through the mouth of a gargoyle, cast in iron – *nice,* I thought, wincing. The gargoyle was also cold to the touch, icy. I rapped hard against the wood.

There was no reply. No sign of life on the other side at all.

"You have got to be shitting me." That was Drew, any patience he might have had gone. "Are you telling me I've come all this way, and he's not even here?"

"*We* have," I reminded him, albeit under my breath. "Not just you."

Mel looked back down the hill, but only briefly. "If Peter

isn't here, the boatman would have known that. He would have said something."

I looked over my shoulder, too. Where was the boatman? I couldn't see him anymore. Was he inside the boathouse, securing the vessel? He must be. Perhaps he even lived on the island, in staff quarters, or whatever they were called. Readily on hand.

All five of us continued to stand there, some getting further annoyed, some upset – was that a tear on Crissy's cheek? I was confused. I had to try again, either rap harder or…

I reached out a second time, avoiding the gargoyle this time, my hand pushing at the door instead, reasoning that there was no need for a lock, not here. It remained steadfast, however, refusing to budge. I tried again, and again, until Tommy came forward.

"Here, let me," he said.

I stepped aside, a bit peeved that he felt he could do better, but it turned out he was right. His shove was almighty, the door not just relenting but bursting wide open.

"Thank fuck," I heard Mel whisper. I looked at her. She was also shivering, suffering as much as Crissy from the cold.

I didn't ruminate over it for too long. We all wanted one thing: to get inside, to find Peter, find out why he wasn't here to greet us.

Christmas. But in the gloomy entrance hall, a wrought iron chandelier remaining unlit, there was no hint of it. It was…austere. It was also impressive, the size of it at least. In Birmingham, my entire flat could have fitted into this space very comfortably indeed.

Drew began circling the room. "Well, bloody hell, would

you look at this?"

The walls were wood panelled, floor to ceiling, the wood on the floor equally dark – walnut, perhaps? Gnarled and knotted. There was a narrow rickety table to one side and on the other wall a couple of chairs, fashioned from dark wood too, and side by side. That was it. Nothing else. Nothing…personal. No pictures hanging from hooks, of ancestors long gone, perhaps, or bright flowers placed in a vase. At the far end, to the right, was a staircase, not that you could see where it led as it was enclosed by more wood panelling.

"Peter!" It was Mel who called out, her voice carrying but not far, as if the room was possessive of it, every door that led off the hall closed. So many doors, I counted five, causing me to think we'd not just entered a house but a Tardis.

I wasn't the only one looking around, Crissy was too, brown eyes wider than ever, her teeth chewing at her lip again. She'd draw blood if she continued to do that, create a big, pulpy mess. I moved a little closer to her.

"Are you okay?" My voice was low, intended only for her.

"This place…" she replied, also whispering.

"I know, it's strange, isn't it?"

She looked at me then. "Strange? Is that what you think? Is that…*all* you think?"

There was no time to ask her what she meant, not with Drew, Tommy and Mel having moved to a door to the right, clearly hellbent on exploring.

Mel reached the door first and pushed it open.

"Whoa," she exclaimed, whilst doing so. "This is some place Petey's got himself, eh?"

I followed them into the room beyond, so did Crissy, I

don't think she did so from curiosity, though, more that she didn't want to be left alone. The room before us was again something splendid, the scale of it. A living room, with three sets of mullioned windows, heavy drapes at them, but kept open, a Chesterfield sofa, a couple of armchairs, a big old stone fireplace and rugs on the wooden floor. No warmth to the room, though, no flames dancing in the grate, and still no personal effects, no photographs, no knick-knacks, bare walls, off-white and cracked in places, cobwebby too, in the corners.

Tommy threw himself down on the Chesterfield, which creaked as if in protest.

"Needs a bit of doing up," he said, spreading his arms and legs wide, "but I'll take it."

Mel, though, was showing signs of disgruntlement. "No bloody Christmas tree."

Drew tutted. "Why d'ya want one for? This is Christmas with a difference, remember?"

"It's that all right," she replied. "Still, better than dinner with the stiffs back home."

"Course it is," Tommy said, eyeing her, eyeing us all. "Peter said there'd be plenty of booze, what say you we go and find it? Get started."

"Too bloody right," said Drew, his lip curled as he snarled, *actually* snarled.

I immediately protested. "We can't just help ourselves. We need to wait for Peter."

Drew turned to face me. "What, we have to worry about his feelings, when he's not worried about ours?"

"But—"

Mel interrupted me. "He's right. We've come all this way, made an effort. The least he can do is what he promised on the invite, and provide for us."

Tommy jumped up from the sofa. "Come on, let's check out the rest of this des res."

Again, Crissy and I had no option but to follow, although the last thing I wanted was to remain in their company a minute longer than necessary.

Crissy was different, however. Crissy I might be able to bear. This slip of a girl who, even though she kept her hands firmly by her side, seemed to cling to me.

Another door led into another room, and so on and so on. I was right about this house being a Tardis, it just kept revealing itself. More living rooms, not as grand as the first, one or two of them snugs, I supposed, all the windows set in stone surrounds, the leading in the glass reminding me of something, of prison bars, creating further unease, a feeling that I was incarcerated, that a sentence had been passed, the terms of which I had yet to discover. Crissy may not have physically clutched onto me, but I found myself reaching out and clutching onto her instead. She looked at me, so many emotions in her eyes, a riot of them, but there was relief too, I was sure of it, that I was as uncomfortable as her.

Finally, we found the kitchen, another vast room, and the heart of the home allegedly, but as the surfaces were bare, almost entirely, it felt anything but.

Whilst Crissy and I stood there, like lost orphans in the storm, the others rummaged around, opening cupboard door after cupboard door, eventually finding the fridge.

"Thank fuck," said Drew. "There's food, some drink too, like he promised."

"You'd think there'd be staff really, wouldn't you, in a house like this?" Mel observed.

"Yeah, where's the maid?" wondered Tommy, that

lopsided grin of his really quite inane. "Nice if she was blonde, and fit. Know what I mean?"

"A cellar. There's bound to be one. There'll be more drink there, maybe even a few vintage numbers, the family treasure so to speak. There'd better be because what's in the fridge won't last long." Drew then turned to us. "Shall we do that? Find the cellar?" He lifted his hands and wiggled his fingers, made a few ghostly shrieking noises that immediately grated on my nerves. "Venture down into the basement, never to return!"

Mel laughed and then shrugged. "As long as there's plenty of wine down there, I wouldn't mind one bit. I'd die happy!"

"Stop it!" Crissy had extricated herself from me and now stood there, a trembling but somehow defiant wreck. "Stop all this talk of death!"

"What?" Mel looked genuinely surprised. "I didn't mean—"

"You shouldn't talk about things like that, not here!"

Tommy and Drew looked at each other. "What the fuck?" Drew muttered.

"Crissy," I said, feeling I had to do something, dampen down a situation that was getting out of hand. When I touched her this time, however, she threw me off, *violently*.

"We've got to be careful!" she continued to shout, to insist. "Very careful."

"What's wrong, Crissy?" I dared to ask as the others stood there gawping. "Can you explain? Help us try to understand?"

From staring at them, she jerked her head towards me, such horror on her face, such... sorrow. "I don't know," she said, desperation in her voice. "Not yet. I just... If Peter's not here, we shouldn't be either. Without Peter..." She stopped and bit her lip again.

I wondered what to do, find the boatman instead of Peter, head back to Anglesey with this girl who was more than just a little uneasy, get a taxi to pick us up, find a B and B somewhere? Sure it was Christmastime, but some were bound to be operating still, although those I'd spied on the way over had looked pretty dead. Even so...

My mind made up, relief surging through me in fact, I addressed her. "Crissy, if you want to go, no problem. I can––"

"Oh. Hello." A voice interrupted me, not booming, but still able to carry well enough. "I...I didn't realise. Sorry. I was upstairs, thought I heard voices. You're here. All of you."

The voice, coming from behind us, caused us all to turn towards it. There wasn't time to ponder the strangeness of his words, not in that instance, only Peter himself. He was not the Peter I remembered – that any of us remembered, I should imagine, a young boy, a lad, with kindness in his eyes. What was in his eyes now was something I couldn't gauge. If not exactly surprised to see us, he was something else, dismayed? He was our age, or thereabouts, but you'd never think it, not now. He could have been ten years older, at least, the skin on his face not smooth anymore, but rough and reddened as if weather-worn, grooves instead of lines that ran from nose to mouth, and hair that was already threaded with grey. He was thin, as fragile as Crissy to look at. But that wasn't the only change in him after all these years. He was in a wheelchair, sitting hunched in it. Not really a man, not in the glare of the kitchen strip light, but a husk instead.

Chapter Five

HARSH. TOO HARSH. Peter was *not* a husk. He was simply unwell, he must be. And living here seemingly on his own, in challenging conditions, clearly wasn't helping.

I forgot about Crissy, forgot about all of them. Instead, I ventured forwards, tentatively, the first one of us to do so, taking the lead again.

"Peter!" I said, with as much enthusiasm as I could muster.

A smile spread across his face, so reluctant that it did something to me, it hurt my heart, when I thought it was hurt enough already.

"Peter," I said again, this time far more gently. "It's good to see you."

He reached out a hand, and I had to say, I hesitated. It looked wafer thin, parched, like the blood below the surface had long since run dry. *Take it, Beth, for God's sake, take it!*

I obeyed my own instruction, felt my skin tingle as we touched, my body judder almost, hoping, praying, he hadn't noticed.

"Thank you," he said.

The fact he didn't return the compliment and say that it

was good to see me too caused me to remember his greeting, or rather lack of one. Had he forgotten we were coming, his illness not just physical but something that also affected his mind?

As we continued to hold hands, there was a moment of silence. I didn't know what else to say and I don't think Peter did either. That moment was shattered, however, as I knew it would be, by the other three, who seemed to rush forward as one.

"Pete, mate, what a pile you've got!"

That was Tommy, quickly followed by Drew.

"Done all right for yourself, haven't you?"

Mel was almost flirtatious, something I bristled at. Peter was obviously ill. Why would she flirt with him? What would be her motive?

"Hey, Peter," his name was a drawl on her lips, "thank you for inviting me here. I just love it. We're going to have ourselves a ball, right?" She then virtually pushed me aside, standing in the very spot I had occupied, bending down and kissing him on his cheek, something that also annoyed me. That she had the guts to do it.

Rather than look at the three of them fawning over Peter, because that's exactly what they were doing, I turned to Crissy. She hadn't moved. She was standing there, observing all that was unfolding, that same bewildered look on her face, that same gnawing of the lip. I think I'm a relatively patient person, but I felt irritated with her, and with myself too. Just what was her problem? What was mine? We'd had an invitation from an old friend to come and stay with him at Christmas, and whether or not he'd forgotten about it, we were here; we should make the best of it. Suddenly, I was determined to do just that. It was an unusual place, but so what? It was still his home, on an island, only a mile off the coast. Not *that* big a deal. People occupied such dwellings; it wasn't like he was the only one. And fair enough, the boatman had been odd too, with his enduring silence, presented to us like some Stygian figure. But this was Wales, *rural* Wales. I'd heard the people were a little different here, fey, even. As for Peter himself and his appearance, maybe he'd explain it in time.

"You'll want to freshen up, won't you?" Peter was saying. "Before dinner, I mean. There are plenty of rooms, I can show you to them."

"Yeah, sure," said Tommy, stifling a yawn. "It has been a bit of a long one."

"How do you…um…" Mel's voice trailed off.

"Manage the stairs?" Peter filled in the gap.

"Well…yeah."

"There's a lift."

"Oh," Mel's laugh sounded far from genuine. "Handy."

He nodded, before adding almost wearily, "There's much to discover."

"Discover? Well…yeah," she said again.

"Soon," he promised.

"What's for dinner?" Tommy said, glancing again at the bare surfaces.

"It'll be as you expect," Peter assured him.

Before showing us to our rooms, though, he addressed the one person in the room who hadn't yet said a word to him. "Crissy," he said. "You're here too."

She didn't answer, only looked at him, and besides fear and confusion, there was a spark of something else in her eyes, just a glimmer before it died out. Anger, was that it? Aimed at whom? Him, for inviting her, or at herself, for accepting?

"You know what?" said Drew, barging his way through the group, towards the fridge again. "I could really use a shower, and then I want a long, hard drink. You got gin?"

Peter had to drag his eyes from Crissy. "Of course. In one of the lower cupboards"

"And tonic or something?"

"Right there in the fridge."

"I'll mix one up, take it to my room."

"Help yourself," Peter replied, his tone again suggesting weariness.

"Anyone else?" said Drew, doing exactly that.

"Hell, yeah!" Mel and Tommy enthused, all three of them now rifling through the cupboards until they found what they needed. If Peter had been able-bodied, would they have acted like this? I wondered. They were practically taking over.

Peter wheeled himself towards a door, the one he'd used to enter the room.

"This house is a bit of a warren," he warned, his eyes on me, not on Crissy. It was like he couldn't *bear* to look at Crissy again. "I'm sure you'll get used to it. In time."

"In time?" I said, smiling and frowning simultaneously. "We've only got four days."

"Time enough," he said.

With drinks in hand, the aroma of gin overpowering, sickly even, able to make my head spin, just the smell of it, the three caught up with us, Drew powering his way into the lead.

"Where's this lift?" he said, one hand pushing at the door.

It didn't lead through to the main entrance hall, which

was what I expected, but a much smaller hall, likely positioned off it. Dark and confined, the walls were once again clad in wood, a couple of wall sconces embedded within the panelling, doing their utmost to shed a degree of light, but failing, causing me at least to squint. There was indeed a lift, concealed behind another door, a set of wrought-iron gates with yet more bars. I peered into the space beyond. Would we all fit?

Peter had no such worries as he opened the gates and waved us in. He then manoeuvred his wheelchair so that he backed into the lift, the rest of us pressing ourselves up against its interior walls.

The gate slid shut, closing us in. I'd been wondering how I'd cope with these people, but now here I was, packed like sardines against them.

The tremor was back in Mel's voice. "Tell me there's only one floor."

"There is," Peter said without turning his head.

Crissy was beside me, shoulder to shoulder. I could feel how stiff she was, how much tension her body contained. As well as Peter, I'd have to speak to her at some point soon, even if it was just to say that I understood her nerves, that I had her back. Maybe when we were shown to our rooms, I'd pop across to hers and do it then. I tried to catch her eye, to convey my intention, but like Peter, she kept staring straight ahead.

Tension. Not only from Crissy. There it was again, emanating from the other three. Drew gulped at his gin, as did Mel and Tommy, just knocking it back. I was sweating, I was sure of it. And yet…the temperature in the house, in this lift, only now I realised, wasn't exactly warm. There was a chill in the air, raw edged, the kind that could sink through layers of clothing, through skin even, to settle deep in your bones.

Mere moments later, the lift ground to a halt, moments that had felt like an age. From now on, I'd take the stairs, not wishing to be confined again.

Peter wheeled himself out, through the gates, and then through a door, and we followed. The corridor we'd emerged into was the darkest shade of black, causing one of us – Crissy maybe, or Mel – to take a sharp intake of breath.

"Jesus Christ," Tommy said, more colourfully. "Where's the bleeding light switch?"

Although Peter hadn't answered, he moved forwards slightly, the wheels on his chair as creaky as the lift, and suddenly there was light. Not much of it, though, just like there hadn't been in that smaller hall, and again it was courtesy of wall sconces rather than a main light, one or two of which flickered, as if they too were cold and shivering.

"Your rooms," Peter said, leading us down the corridor, long and narrow, which wrapped around the corner to reveal yet another. At a door on the right, he stopped.

He looked up at us, seemed to assess us, before speaking again. "Tommy," he said. "You can have this room."

"Great!" Tommy enthused, bounding forward, some of the gin spilling. His rucksack was over his shoulder; he hitched it up before trying the door, which wouldn't budge.

"You'll need this," said Peter, rifling in his pocket before extracting a key.

"Oh right, thanks," Tommy replied. "Didn't realise we were gonna need keys. Someone thinking of coming bursting in, are they? Mel, what about you, eh?"

Mel guffawed as hard as Tommy. "Maybe," she returned, holding up her drink. "Depends how much of this you can get down me!"

Peter didn't comment on the tawdry exchange, just held the key aloft. Tommy took it and inserted it into the lock, had to struggle to get it to turn, before opening the door. Inside was the same degree of darkness we'd encountered after the lift, making him falter.

I didn't blame him, not this time. The room resembled a yawning chasm.

"Next," said Peter, leaving Tommy still hovering on the threshold.

"Hang on a minute," Tommy called. "What time are we meeting downstairs? I'm starved."

"Dinner is at seven," Peter informed him. The four of us glanced at Tommy, noting the agitation on his face, in his voice, before we duly followed our host.

Mel's was the room along from Tommy, on the same side, Drew further down on the left. As for Crissy and me, we were led to another corridor, only to find more darkness.

A whimper escaped Crissy.

"Peter, where are the lights?" I said, wishing to appease her.

"Here," he replied, again moving forwards and flicking a switch, a switch like the other one, that was at wheelchair level, the house adapted to suit his needs.

"Not far now," Peter insisted, moving again. "I've put you close to each other."

"Oh, that's good, isn't it, Crissy?" I said, but if I thought she might show that she was happy about that too, I was wrong. Rather, her eyes were darting all over the place, as if searching. But searching for what? Shadows?

"Peter," I said, "where's your room?"

"Mine?"

"Yes."

"Just along from here," was all the answer he gave.

More silence, the atmosphere was thick with it. Who was going to be allocated the next room? It was like we were picking straws or something. Who'd draw the short one?

"Crissy," he said finally. "This is yours."

He held up the key but she didn't take it, not at first. She stared at it.

"Crissy," I ventured, "I can come in with you if you like--"

Any more words were swallowed as she reached out, grabbed the key, turned her back on us and inserted it into the lock. Standing on the threshold, as Tommy had done, she faced us again. Furious. Bloody furious! Anger giving soft features such a pinched look.

"I'll see you at dinner," she said, before slamming the door.

Chapter Six

THE BEDROOM. OH Christ, the bedroom!

Entering it had indeed been like entering a void. For a moment I was unsure if there *was* anything beyond the threshold, that I'd step over it and fall into nothing, keep on falling, never to emerge. My hand flailing for the light switch, I should have relaxed when I found it and light beat back the gloom – that silly notion dispelled – but I remained uptight.

A large room, the walls were off-white, just as they were downstairs, still with no pictures of any sort to relieve the otherwise bland expanse. A rug had been thrown over wooden floorboards, hand-woven in somewhere as exotic as Persia, perhaps, with the brightest of threads. Now, though, it was dull. Reds, golds and blues as faded as the house itself, as its lone occupant. The bed, not unexpectedly, dominated the room, the ancient frame a plain dark wood, the bedding another grubby shade of white. The mattress, when I tested it, was as hard as stone. The room also housed a chest of drawers, and a bedside table with a lamp. Other than that, there was nothing. Like a monk's room, a monk's *cell*. There was a radiator, one of those old-fashioned bulky things that some people think are trendy and have deliberately installed.

It wasn't trendy in this setting, but rusty and awkward. Walking over to it, I placed my hands against the cast iron to check if it was on. I did this because of the chill in the room, colder than elsewhere in the house. It *was* on, pumping out the heat, the water inside it gurgling at my touch. One step away, however, and any warmth was absent.

Unwelcoming. That's what this room was.

I glanced towards Crissy's bedroom beyond the wall. Was she doing as I was? Standing in her room and just gazing around her, lifting her arms to hug herself, trying to get warm. More to the point, was she thinking as I was? The same kind of thoughts. I would go to her, but that slam of the door, it had been so final.

Desperate to do something other than stand there, I made my way to the window instead. There were curtains hanging there, deep red faded to pink in places, velvet but not plush, not anymore.

I shivered. There was nothing normal about this house, this set-up. Nothing homely.

More darkness awaited me at the window. The island, the house, was steeped in it. I couldn't make out any variations in the land, or how close this side of the house was to the sea, if indeed it was. Just a mile from civilisation. I'd told myself that many times since I'd arrived. Not a million miles. But now, more than ever, it felt like it. Felt like a punishment. My breath misted the glass as I stood there. Of course it wasn't a punishment! What for?

It was an accident!

After Crissy had slammed the door on us and disappeared inside her room, I'd turned to Peter, but he was already creaking onwards in his wheelchair, arms pumping those wheels towards the next bedroom, mine, whereupon he'd handed over yet another key. I'd taken it from him, felt the weight of it in my hand, a cold, hard thing, a relic from the past.

"I thought only hotels had keys," I'd said, just to be conversational, "not regular houses."

"It's for your peace of mind," Peter had replied, eyes averted from mine.

I'd shrugged. "I suppose you're right. These corridors all look similar; it'd be easy to get confused. The others might not mind barging in on each other, but I wouldn't want that."

Still his head hung low. "No, you wouldn't."

"Peter," I'd said, willing him to look at me. Rather than continue, I'd waited until he'd lifted his head, slowly, reluctantly. "I never thought..." I'd nodded back the way we'd come, "you'd have friends like that."

A frown had caused yet more lines on his face. "*My* friends?"

I was taken aback that he was acting surprised again. "Well, yeah. They're not mine!"

"Aren't they?"

"No, Peter," I'd answered, gently but firmly, "they're not. You *do* know them, don't you? They seem to know you."

He seemed to have to fight to clear his head. "Yes. Yes. Of course," he'd said, adding, "I'm very tired." I'd believed him, wholeheartedly, he looked exhausted.

"I'm sorry, Peter."

"I know," came another enigmatic reply. "I know you are."

There had been more silence between us. I'd wondered

56

if I should come right out with it and ask what was wrong with him, what type of illness he suffered from. Would it be too rude, insensitive?

"Crissy's different, though," I'd said instead. "Not like the other three."

"What do you mean?"

God, he'd made me work for any ounce of insight. "She's not like them. Not like me either." I'd given a short laugh before lowering my voice, just in case Crissy was behind her door, had her ear pressed to it. "She seems fragile. Vulnerable. How d'you know her?"

Again, he'd hung his head, his body hunched over, as if folding in on itself.

"Peter?" I'd continued, seeking an answer of some sort. *Needing* it.

Finally, he'd lowered his hands to the wheels and steered away from me.

"I'll see you at dinner," he'd called back.

As I stared after him, I'd made excuses. It was because he was so tired that he was acting this way, tired *and* ill. It was me who'd exhausted him, quizzing him so intently. There'd be answers to all of it; I just had to be patient.

A few minutes later, as I stood in that bedroom, looking about me, out of the window too, at a house, at an island, devoid of personality, warmth and normality, I couldn't help but wonder about the night ahead. I was a stranger amongst strangers in the strangest of places. What lay in store?

Imagination, how it can run away with you!

The dinner, held downstairs that evening in a long, narrow strip of dining room, sandwiched between one of the living rooms and the kitchen, was actually nowhere near as bad as I'd feared it was going to be. Not just feared it, I'd dreaded it.

Seven o'clock was the time Peter had said to attend, time in which to put aside my musings and get ready. There was a small en suite bathroom attached to my room, nothing fancy, as I was coming to expect, rather it was plain and functional, containing a bath with shower, sink, and toilet. A mirror was over the sink, one that became clouded in steam as soon as I turned on the hot tap. Even when I rubbed at the mirror and tried to see my reflection in it, it was virtually impossible. A glimpse was all I managed, enough to notice how tired and strained I looked before the glass was fogged yet again.

I didn't linger in the bathroom to enjoy a long, hot soak, but instead hurried to get out of there, feeling the weight of enclosure, just as I had in the lift, in this entire house actually, and on the island too. A little before seven, I left my room and entered the corridor, wondering if I should stop outside Crissy's room and rap on her door. I hung around for a short while, listening for any sign of life from within, but all was still. So still that I carried on without her, past more flickering wall lights, ignoring the shadow they cast upon the walls – *my* shadow, that followed me determinedly.

In the corridor that housed Tommy, Drew and Mel, I didn't want to loiter at all, quickly rounding the corner into the first corridor we'd encountered, one that was yet again in full darkness. Oh, how long it seemed, like a tunnel of some sort, the end unseen and therefore endless. I had to venture down it, but I couldn't help but feel reluctant, as if I'd wind up wandering down it forever, trying to find my way out but continually failing.

I needed light. All would be okay if there was light.

My hand searching the wall, I eventually found it, remembering to bend slightly in order to locate it. Flicking the switch, nothing happened. It remained dark. I pressed it again and again. Still nothing. *Shit!* The wiring was clearly faulty, so what should I do? Retrace my footsteps, perhaps, knock for the other three. What if they were downstairs already? No way would they want to waste a minute of valuable drinking time.

I should just get on with it, put one foot in front of the other and force myself onwards. There were more doors on either side of me. Was one room Peter's? What else lay behind them? Just bedrooms. *Empty* bedrooms, although I couldn't help but think otherwise. Not full of ghosts. I'm not stupid. Full of…history. That was a better way to put it. Four walls soaked with the thoughts and emotions of those that had once occupied them. Heavy thoughts, like mine had been earlier. Thoughts that could send you mad if you let them. Had that happened here? Had the silence, the sheer loneliness, amplified the voices in past residents' heads, those voices we all have, that nag, that tell us how different we are, how worthless, until all resistance broke down, and sanity fled? It was too easy to imagine, to visualise in my mind's eye the residue of these people, strangers again, becoming shadows, like the one following me, full of grief, anger, hatred even.

Shadows that would reach out, that would recognise me…

I should run down that long, long corridor, as fast as I could. Close my eyes, for what difference would it make? Get it over and done with.

But I couldn't move an inch. It was as if I was paralysed. I continued to stand there, beads of sweat forming on my forehead, despite the ever-pervading chill, my breath becoming harder, faster. What was in those rooms?

"Beth?"

At the sound of my name, I emitted a scream and spun round on my heel.

"Beth, what the fuck?"

Along with the sound of Mel's voice, there was light.

"How did you…?"

Mel shrugged. "How did I what?"

I struggled to form words. "The light. I tried. Wouldn't work."

She shrugged again and pointed to the switch. "Works fine for me." She strode forwards, confidently, purposefully. "Come on, let's get going. I need another drink, plus I'm starving. Let's hope the kitchen fairies have been hard at work."

It turned out they'd been industrious indeed. When we arrived downstairs a few minutes later, Mel having linked arms with me, practically dragging me down that corridor to the staircase, which wound its way innocently enough back to the ground floor, there was a smell in the air, quite delicious actually, making me realise I was hungry too. At the bottom of the stairs, Mel broke away.

"Where's the fucking dining room?" she muttered, but it was good-naturedly enough. "This house is so big, you need signposts!"

As she searched, opening door after door, I trailed behind

her, glancing over my shoulder at the stairs only once before we entered another room, wondering about those lights, about the terror I'd experienced which seemed so distant now, plain daft. This was a house. An old house, admittedly, with history, and in an unusual location, but for all that, still just a house, bricks and mortar. If I was going to survive for the next few days I'd better keep a tight rein on my thoughts and the rabbit holes they disappeared down.

Survive? There I went again, being dramatic.

Still hot on Mel's heels, we found ourselves in one of the snugs. "Nope, not here," Mel muttered again, locating another door at the far end of it. That led us into a room similar to the last – just how many rooms did one family need? Eventually, though, she yanked open another door, impatience beginning to show in her grasp, and there it was, the dining room. Around a laden table, which was as long and as narrow as the corridors, sat Tommy, Drew and Crissy, with Peter at the helm.

"Thank God," Mel said, as Tommy raised a tumbler in greeting, filled to the brim with more gin, I suspected. "Pour me one, would you?"

He duly obeyed, and she took it from him, seating herself beside him too whilst eyeing everything on offer. "This is more like it," she continued. "This'll do me nicely."

I sat too, next to Crissy, Drew asking me if I wanted some wine. I nodded, and he poured some red, which I thanked him for. I couldn't help but wonder about the food – roasted meats, potatoes and vegetables, all on silver platters – where had it come from? We'd been in our rooms for a couple of hours, and during that time, Peter had whipped up all this? We'd seen no sign of prep in the kitchen and no sign of a resident chef, either. Maybe it was the boatman. Maybe he doubled as a cook or something. Who knew? Why question it? Question everything? Why couldn't I do as the others did, some of them at least, and just enjoy myself? 'Tis the season after all, damned or not. There might be no Christmas decorations in the dining room, no adornments of any kind, but before us was a feast worthy of any occasion.

That night, the wine flowed, the gin, the vodka, the rum, all available in copious amounts. Even Crissy drank a few glasses of wine, lost something of that haunted look, her shoulders easing a little, although she still kept looking around her, behind and far ahead down the long room, chewing at her lips or her nails every time she did.

The conversation also flowed. We got to know how each of us had met Peter. At work, or through friends, that kind of thing. Soon enough, though, talk turned to the elephant in the room.

I might not have had the courage to come straight out and ask Peter about his disability during that brief time we were alone upstairs, but Drew, it seemed, had no such qualms.

"So come on then, tell us what happened with your legs," he said, a slur in his voice. "How you ended up on wheels."

Just his legs? I wanted to say. *What about Peter in general? Look how much he's aged!*

Peter shrugged, a fork in his hand, with which he pushed food around the plate. He'd barely eaten a thing, I noticed, or touched his wine.

"It's just one of those things," he said.

"What things?" Mel asked, not looking particularly interested to be honest, as she poured yet another gin, making a dent in a sizeable bottle.

Peter had answered quite a few questions over the course

of the dinner. *How long have you been here?* Not long, a year or so. *You on your own?* Yes. *Don't you get lonely?* Occasionally. *Bored?* Not really. *Do you have people visit?* Sometimes. *No need to work anymore, eh, Pete?* I wouldn't say that. *So you must be loaded?* I get by. But regarding questions about his health, he was even more vague.

Still Drew persisted. "Whatever you've got, it's not catching, is it?"

At this, Tommy dissolved into gales of laughter, Mel too, the noise they were making reverberating around the narrow room, bouncing off every wall.

Worried for Peter, I would have said something, would have intervened, told the three of them not to be so bloody rude, to show a bit of courtesy to our host who'd gone to so much effort tonight, but Drew then picked up his glass, red wine sloshing over the edges and declared he was only joking 'mate'. "Here's to you, Pete. Cheers for the invite."

And just like that, the moment was lost, no chance for a reprimand at all. At Drew's behest, we all picked up our glasses and held them high, even Crissy, who really was drinking quite a bit of white, keeping up with the others. Not a bad first night. Normal. Almost. What people did, particularly at this time of year. They ate, drank and were merry.

The party broke up around midnight with people rising and making their way back to their rooms. I looked forward to some rest, and some privacy too. I was tired, but I was also drunk, more than I'd realised, the room momentarily swaying as I too pushed aside the dining room chair and stood up. I was surprised at myself. I never drank like this, rarely socialised, not for years and years. It was a feeling I wasn't used to but which I found I quite liked. How the alcohol made everything dream-like.

As I negotiated the stairs and that first corridor again, the lights having remained on this time but so damned low, I squared my shoulders defiantly. I would *not* be frightened again, and by absolutely nothing. I wouldn't be like Crissy. Crissy, who had barely said a word at dinner, just continued drinking. Only Peter had abstained. But so what? Big deal.

Whatever gets you through the night…

Well if it did that, it was worth it.

Chapter Seven

THE NEXT MORNING, I woke with the mother of all headaches, and something else, a stone in the pit of my stomach, something that was round and hard, and refused to shift. I sighed. If I'd felt relaxed the evening before, it hadn't lasted long. Perhaps I'd need to spend the next three days in an alcoholic haze in order to cope. But just as quickly, I dismissed the notion. That wasn't the answer, no matter what I might have thought.

I sat up in bed, wondering when I'd get proper time alone with Peter. It would be good to talk more deeply with him, find out how he knew my address, how hard he'd dug.

It was as I swung my legs over the bed, my feet touching that threadbare rug, not soft beneath my feet, rougher than floorboards actually, that I heard them, voices drifting towards me, their volume increasing. What was going on? Grabbing a jumper from the end of the bed, one I'd discarded in my drunken stupor, I pulled it on, shivering as I did so, before heading into the corridor. The voices were from further away, from the other corridor, and so I hurried towards them, towards Mel, Tommy and Drew's rooms.

"Why are you whispering outside my door? You did it during the night as well."

It was Drew, lambasting Tommy.

Tommy denied it. "I didn't do anything. I was sparked out. What are you talking about?"

"It *was* you! You were outside my door and kept whispering stuff. Weird…stuff. Stuff about me. I shouted out, told you to shut the fuck up. And now you've started up again, a few minutes ago."

"Are you on one, mate? I did no such thing."

Mel also emerged from her room as I approached, her look of fury matching Drew's.

"Did you keep banging on the wall, Tommy? 'Cos I heard several big thumps in the night, all coming from the direction of your bedroom. If I hadn't been so drunk I'd have gone to your room and lamped you one."

"What?" Tommy was even more incredulous. "Don't be so stupid!"

Her fury increased. "Stupid? Me? I'm not the one who's fucking stupid!"

If Tommy was guilty, he was doing a good job of appearing otherwise. "Why are you all blaming me? I've done nothing!"

"It was you, Tommy!" Drew insisted.

"And it was your side of the wall those thumps were coming from," added Mel.

Drew became even more aggressive. "Do you think you're being funny, mate? Trying to scare us. Trying to pretend that there are ghosts here, or something? Think you can get away with that fucking behaviour, do you? That you're what…cleverer than us? 'Cos you ain't. You really ain't. We're not going to put up with your shit."

I was aghast, listening to them. Stunned by how quickly the situation was deteriorating, just becoming…nasty. And over what? A bit of tomfoolery. Either that or imagination.

I hurried further along the corridor. It was too early for this nonsense, just after nine. No one had spotted me yet; they were too busy accusing each other. By the time I reached them, Drew had backed Tommy up against the wall, had raised an arm as well, his fist bunched. Mel was standing by, staring, but no longer saying anything. She didn't have to; her expression spoke volumes. There was glee in it, her eyes practically burning with excitement. *Do it! Do it! Do it!*

Drew was pulling his arm back, inch by inch, as if enjoying the effect such an action was having on Tommy, who had started to gibber.

"Drew!" I shouted. "What the hell? Get away from him. Just… Step back!"

What happened next was odder still.

Tommy had been focused entirely on Drew, Drew entirely on Tommy, Mel on Drew, but then all three shifted their gaze towards me, and for a moment, there was no recognition at all in their eyes, as if I was someone they'd never seen before, not spent an entire evening with. A total stranger, yet again.

"It's me!" I felt compelled to say. "Beth. And you've got to stop, all three of you. Now."

Even stranger, recognition took time to resurface.

"Drew!" I said again, and slowly, gradually, he lowered his fist, blinking all the while.

Some of the tension drained from Tommy too, and Mel had lowered her head, was shaking it from side to side.

I stepped forward. "What's all this about whispering and banging on walls?"

"What?" Mel said, much to my amazement.

"You were all just having a go at Tommy because of it, accusing him."

"I've done nothing," Tommy repeated, his lower lip trembling.

"Drew," I said, "Tommy's pretty sure he's not guilty of anything, maybe you ought to back off."

Drew did indeed back off, putting a few steps between them both.

"I heard whispering," he said, hanging his head, almost close to tears himself. "At my door. A voice. Muffled, but… It must have been his! In the night. I thought it was just…I don't know, I was drunk, I put the pillow over my head and went back to sleep. This morning, though, whoever it was, was at it again. They were saying things."

"What things?" I said, unable to deny my curiosity. Had this really happened?

"Just…things. It was as if…as if they knew me. The *real* me. Judging me. Threatening me." Drew raised a hand to wipe at his eyes. Shit! He *was* crying. He was really affected by this. Mel too was pale, not crying, but not her usual bolshie self, her auburn hair awry.

"I promise it wasn't me!" Tommy said again. "I like a bit of a joke, but…not this."

Drew turned on him again, such fury in his voice. "How'd I know you're telling the truth? I don't know you from Adam, do I? You're a fucking stranger, mate. *His* friend. Not mine."

At the mention of Peter, he appeared, wheeling himself around the corner

"Problem?" he said, his voice raspy, a bad night's sleep having taken its toll, perhaps.

No one said anything, not even me. In fairness, I didn't

know what to say. Also, I couldn't shake the thought that Peter was being disingenuous. That he'd been waiting just out of sight, had heard everything, and therefore knew full well there was a problem. If it was a male responsible for the supposed whisperings, could it be Peter and not Tommy? What about the thumps on the wall, heard by Mel, but coming from Tommy's room? Sounds travel, though, and in a house as big as this, they could travel far indeed, they could echo. Had he invited us here to toy with us? Was this some sort of game?

The silence endured, until eventually I had to say something, wanting to get the whole debacle over with. "Nothing's wrong," I said. "It's sorted."

"Good," Peter said, attempting a smile, but not one that reached his eyes. "Breakfast will be ready in an hour in the dining room. I'll see you then."

He continued wheeling past us, to the lift I presumed. Tommy also moved. "I'm going to my room," he muttered.

Drew and Mel followed suit, Drew's nostrils still flaring, leaving me alone in the corridor once again, my eyes travelling towards the far end of it, where there was a window. There was light outside, but it was weak, a cloudy day then, maybe even with some drizzle in the air. What the hell were we going to do in such weather on an island like this? How were we going to pass the day? Hours and hours seemed to stretch ahead of me, my sense of dread increasing. Hours spent with strangers – *volatile* strangers.

I started walking back to my room, and as I did, another sound caught my attention, that of a door shutting. Not Tommy, or Drew, or Mel's door, they'd already been opened then slammed shut, but that of a door just ahead of me. Crissy's? Her room was right next to mine. If I'd heard a commotion, then she must have too. She'd come out of her room, but then returned back inside. A second noise followed, that of the key in the lock as it scraped its way round the barrel.

Like Peter, she was hiding from us.

Breakfast was a strained affair. Everyone had shown up, even Crissy, the table cleared of debris from the night before, not that we'd helped I realised, none of us had, we'd just…left it there, for Peter, and maybe the elusive boatman. Something I now felt bad about. I'd have to rectify that, pull my weight.

We took our places, Drew somewhat sheepish, but there was anger still. As for Mel, she was almost as edgy as Crissy, and Tommy's cheeky chappy persona had disappeared entirely. I may have broken the fight up earlier, but resentments simmered.

Someone had to make conversation, though, because the silence was stifling. It was a simple breakfast that had been provided, nothing like the grand scale of dinner the night before. Rather, an assortment of cereals had been laid out, toast, butter, and jams. The coffee had all been poured and so I grabbed the cafetière and rose from my chair, offering to make more.

At once, Peter shook his head. "No! I'll do it."

"It's no problem—"

"You're my guests," he said, holding his hand out for the cafetière.

"But—"

"And I can manage perfectly well."

A pride thing. Maybe that's what it was. I held my peace and sat back down, watched him make his way towards the door and push it open.

Still silence.

"Crissy," I said. "Did you sleep well?"

"Yes."

How low and breathy her voice was, a whisper in it.

"So…um…I've forgotten. How did you say you knew Peter again?"

She'd been gazing downwards at a plate empty of any food, but now her head came abruptly up, and she turned to look at me. "I've always known him."

"Oh!" I was surprised. Clearly Mel was too, as she was looking at Crissy quizzically.

"Were your parent's friends, or something?" I continued.

"Not really."

"Have you visited the island before?"

"No."

"But you kept in touch?"

"Not recently, no."

Just as abruptly, she stared downwards again, signalling the conversation was over, with her at least.

I tried to remember the details of the conversation from the previous night, but found I couldn't, probably because of the drink I'd consumed, and so I asked the others too, whether they'd kept in regular touch with Peter, sure that like me and like Crissy, they were friends from his past, not the present.

Drew was the first to answer, in between stuffing toast into his mouth. "Haven't seen him in bloody years, mate," adding with a cruel burst laughter, "why would I?"

Mel smirked at his reply, incredibly. Even Tommy laughed, a shower of crumbs spraying from his mouth, the only thing to decorate the table. There they were again, the three amigos, united by that trait they all shared, their arrogance. What was it with their attitude? I wondered. They'd known Peter, but they hadn't kept in touch, didn't seem to want to, seemed contemptuous of him in fact, and yet, despite that, all three had accepted an invitation to come and spend Christmas with him. Why? For the free ride? The food and the drink? Parasites, that's what they were, always seeking to enjoy themselves at someone else's expense. What had happened this morning, however, hadn't been enjoyable for anyone. Too extreme to be brushed aside like it was.

The door opened again and Peter entered, clutching a full cafetière.

"Here you are," he said, approaching the table and placing it down there. Just before he did, though, I noticed something else about him, how his hand was shaking, black coffee, like mud, splashing over the brim of the glass and dripping down its exterior.

I'd worried about how to occupy the hours before, and again that worry resurfaced. Last night might have been bearable, but today, so far, *this morning*, had been torturous.

I tried again to kick-start a conversation, approaching a more general topic this time.

"What's back on the mainland?" I asked. "I remember reading about this part of Wales, Anglesey's supposed to be beautiful, isn't it? I was thinking about a day trip there."

Peter had just repositioned himself at the head of the table and was reaching forward, perhaps for a piece of toast, but his hand stopped in mid-air.

"What are you talking about?" he said, sounding almost as breathless as Crissy.

Before answering him, I glanced at Crissy. Hope had flared in her eyes when I'd suggested a day trip, but when Peter spoke, it fled. "I just thought there'd be lots to explore."

Peter was as incredulous as Tommy earlier. "But you haven't explored the island yet!"

"The island isn't big, though," I countered, trying not to sound rude. "And I don't know about the tides, but do they ever come this far out? Is it possible to walk to the mainland?"

He didn't answer that question, seemed to accuse me instead. "You wanted to escape."

I was the one taken aback now. "Escape Christmas you mean?"

Peter nodded emphatically. "You wouldn't have come here otherwise."

"What? I might have done—"

Still he wouldn't let me speak. "Everything you need is here. Everything."

Mel had stopped eating, was drinking more coffee instead. "A library. Surely a house like this has got a library?" she said.

Peter swung his head towards her. "Yes! Yes, there is one."

"So you've got plenty of books?" she continued. "I like reading. Crime mainly, fiction or non-fiction, I don't mind." She looked at me then. "Do you like crime too?"

My face burned. Was that a dig or something? Did she know? I then turned to Peter. Did he know, and he'd told her? Told them all. And now I was the one being judged.

Paranoia. It was always there, a viper waiting to strike. I had to take a deep breath, albeit surreptitiously. So what if they knew. It was an accident. Just a fucking accident!

I continued to eye Peter, who quickly lowered his head. There was to be no trip to Anglesey, but hey, there was a library, somewhere in this mad jumble of rooms. There'd be more drinking too, no doubt about it, although maybe not so much on my part, and more eating. Christmas with a difference. How that had appealed a few short days ago with the prospect of the office Christmas party looming, after which I'd return home to that tiny flat, which in its way, I realised, was as impersonal as this house, a place in which to exist but nothing more. Another season spent alone whilst outside my door the world functioned normally. I remembered how I had felt on opening Peter's invite. It was like a gift, the best Christmas present ever, because he'd saved me from it all. I was grateful.

Now, though, as I replenished my coffee cup, having been refused – literally refused – exit from the island, my hand was shaking too.

Chapter Eight

JUST LIKE PEOPLE had dispersed after dinner the previous evening, so they did after breakfast…just got up from the table and disappeared.

As Peter began transporting empty dishes to the kitchen, I at least offered to help rather than scuttle away.

"Let me see to things," he said, once again refusing. "I prefer it."

For a while, I continued to sit there, watching as he worked, wishing he'd just stop and talk to me, really talk, answer the questions that I had – *how did you find me? How long have you lived here? What's really wrong with you, Peter? Is it…terminal?*

The latter was something I knew I couldn't ask, along with another question that played on my mind: *how can you stand to live here alone?* In a house that was so huge, so cold, *so hostile*. It was exactly that. I'd been invited here, had black and white proof of it, and yet now I realised it was a mistake. A big one. On the bright side, one night was gone, just three more to go, and then we'd be ferried back across that murky sea. Christmas would be over, or as good as. What came after was something I'd also need to tackle.

I continued to dwell on these thoughts as I finally left the dining room, intending to do as Peter had suggested and go outside and explore. Having returned to my room only briefly to grab my coat and swap shoes for boots, I then hurried back down those dark corridors as quickly as I'd hurried up them, still disliking so many locked doors on either side of me, before descending the staircase and reaching the entrance hall. There I levered open that big old oak door with its gargoyle knocker, the latter like something from a Dickens novel, that would change if you stared at it, come hideously to life.

Outside, I made my way further down the path, pulling my coat tighter whilst wondering if I might bump into one of the others, if they'd had the same idea as me.

There was no one, though. Only me. The island was as desolate as its name suggested – Anghyfannedd. I'd have to ask Peter about that too, when, *if*, I got the chance, whether it really was something the locals called it, or the island's official name. If just a nickname, I'm not sure it made it any more palatable. Having kept to the path so far, I steered away from it, to the left of the house, what grass there was on this rock soft beneath my feet. I looked around, at the landscape and at the expanse of sea that surrounded me – foamy waves lapping at the shore's edge. There was the mainland, just over there, but it was so removed, alien almost. I'd asked about the tides and whether they ever went so far out that you could walk from island to shore, but somehow I doubted it. We'd need the boat, which was down there, tucked away in the boathouse. A lifeline.

Rather than head to the boathouse, I trudged upwards towards the crest of the island where the cliffs were, walking on and on, the landscape not changing much, nothing to really break it up or give it any colour or interest. Even the surrounding sea was the same thing on repeat, not blue, not in this weather, or at this time of year, but pale and sludgy, as if all colour and joy had been leached from it.

For half an hour I rambled by the edge of the cliffs, surprised at how tall they were and how they cascaded down to the shore. I was beginning to enjoy myself, actually, my solitary situation familiar and comfortable. There was nothing, absolutely nothing, to disturb me. In fact, as I glanced up at a sky that was as colourless as the sea, incessant drizzle falling from the clouds that dominated it, I could still see no evidence of any type of bird. I was alone, quite alone. *We* were, the six of us. Or seven, if the boatman was indeed lurking somewhere. Who cared if he was? I didn't. Up here, even further removed from the world and all who populated it, all cares fell away as if they had never existed in the first place. I felt peace. *Perfect* peace. A glimmer of it that grew in strength, and that brought tears to my eyes because it had been so long since I'd last felt it, if indeed I ever had. I was greedy for it, wanting it to last, to stretch for eternity. Go on and on.

All too soon, though, I was on my way back, almost as if my feet had moved of their own accord, dragging me from the island's only sweet spot to somewhere far less appealing. There it was, in the distance, the house, kept at arm's length for the best part of an hour or so, but in reality, always there, always waiting.

Those people… Peter… The house itself… I had to bolster myself to face them again, talk myself round: *it's just for a few more days. No big deal. Stop making it into one.* I could always spend a large part of my time outside, weather permitting, wrap up well, treading over the same ground, no chore at all if it produced the same feeling.

I was drawing even closer. The island had a name, supposedly, but not the house, not as far as I knew at any rate. As if it didn't deserve one. Instantly, I shook my head. *What a strange thing to think.* Understandable, though, perhaps. A name was personal; it gave a building character, some warmth even. This building held no warmth at all.

I slowed to a halt, continued to examine it, delaying the inevitable.

The back was plainer than the front, with rows and rows of windows on both the upper and lower levels, a chimneystack to one side that looked precarious but belched no smoke. The unrelenting uniformity of the building reminded me of something, something I'd seen in a book perhaps, or whilst browsing online, another type of structure, something very old-fashioned. An asylum? Was that it? Such a comparison made me gasp. This was *not* an asylum, merely a home. Despite reassuring myself of that, I thought again of all those rooms I'd passed and how I'd wondered who they'd belonged to, generations of Bexan family members, also how I'd imagined each of them slowly going mad behind those doors, that madness subsequently becoming something inherent, a trait that couldn't, *wouldn't,* be denied. Because of them, the house had developed an appetite for madness, needing new misfits to gorge on. Hence why we'd been invited…

I couldn't stop the crazy direction in which my mind was careering.

Those windows… They were so dark, every one of them, so empty. Or were they? Because the more I looked, squinted in fact, craning my neck forwards, the more *alive* they seemed. Were those figures at the windows? Not just one or two windows, but all of them. An impossible amount, blackened shapes that stared at me every bit as hard as I was staring at them, although I couldn't see the whites of their eyes, not from here, nothing that would give relief to the darkness of them.

There were figures! Desperate things crammed side by side, jostling with one another, as if in a frenzy, as if trying to break free.

I took a step back, staggered in fact. I wanted to close my eyes, block out such a curious, such an appalling spectacle, and yet they remained open, and I continued to stare. Who were these people, if they could be called that? For I was doubting it, and doubting my sanity too. What was this house doing to me?

Something changed, uncoordinated behaviour became more organised, those figures, those shapes, standing back, some of them at least, and doing something other than jostling. They were pointing at me. Yes! Yes, that was it. Pointing…accusingly.

A sob burst from me. Guttural. Wretched.

Why were they pointing? What did they mean by it?

Did they know?

"It was just an accident!"

I spat the words, hurled them at the shadows, in bitter retaliation. Still they pointed, more and more of them, and all at me. A world of hands.

I could bear it no longer. Shutting my eyes at last, I fell to my knees, a figure of despair too. We all were. Washed up on this lonely, far off island.

How long I stayed like that I had no idea, huge sobs engulfing me. At some point, I must have exhausted the well and opened my eyes.

The house was there, unrepentant, the windows as

uniform as ever.

And empty now.

Completely.

I stood up, dusted myself down, and tried to pull myself together.

That moment of peace, on the crest of the island, how fleeting it was, how distant. I longed for it again, more than ever, wondered if I should turn around and head back there, anything to keep delaying going inside again. Eventually, I decided against it. It was around midday – I had no watch on, so didn't know for sure. Plus, I was discovering that time was different on the island, as if it didn't follow the normal constraints, as if it really was – as some would have you believe – meaningless. Morning, noon and night, it all felt the same. There was a mist rolling in off the sea, not quite reaching the island or mainland yet, but it would, temperatures consequently plummeting further.

No more stalling. I had to get back, feeling exposed suddenly, even more vulnerable. Now that the coast was clear, those figures mere imaginings, I'd be fine inside. I would.

I endeavoured to keep my eyes averted as I drew closer, but the house kept drawing them back, like something magnetic. Those windows may be empty, but they were blackened, every one of them, like the house itself, the true nature of it.

The true nature of me.

Earlier I'd considered the house unwelcoming. That I'd made a grave mistake in coming here, that I shouldn't have.

Now, though, another thought emerged.

I was *exactly* where I was supposed to be.

We all were.

Chapter Nine

"HEY, LOOK WHAT the wind's blown in."

I'd entered the house, discarded my coat and boots and had padded through the entrance hall in socked feet trying to find the library. Regarding my thoughts and my feelings, I was working hard to make sense of them, in effect to overcome, maybe even disregard them. The kind of solitude that existed on the island left you with little else to do but think. A book was what I needed, any type of book, I didn't particularly care, something that would provide an escape of a different sort.

Meandering from one (thankfully) empty room to another, I'd eventually found the library, which wasn't empty. Mel was in there occupying a window seat, a book in her hands, but not one she'd been reading when I entered the room, she'd been staring out the window instead. I winced. As this room overlooked the back of the house, maybe her eyes had been on me beforehand, and she had seen the spectacle I'd made of myself.

"Enjoy your walk, did you?" she continued.

The amusement in her voice confirmed it – she *had* seen. Refusing to bite back, to explain, I simply nodded before crossing over to a series of shelves that covered not one but two walls, top to bottom, to peruse the books there. Dusty tomes, all of them, nothing apparently modern, copies were bound in either leather or sitting in dust jackets. Authors I'd never heard of either and titles that seemed peculiar, non-fiction most of them.

"Which book did you choose?" I said, swinging back round to face Mel.

She was watching me still, eyes boring into me, as if trying to see what lay within.

She took a moment to answer, then shrugged.

"Just some old nonsense on ancient religions, can't get my head around it to be honest. The Pagan kind, you know what I mean? Druids and shit. Don't understand it. Don't really want to. Don't believe in any kind of God, not one bit." She then glanced at the book as if it was covered in maggots or something. "As libraries go, this is pretty piss poor."

That might be so, but I needed something to occupy my mind, to transport me, and so I turned back to the books, not liking the weight of her stare, trying to ignore it as I trailed one finger against the rows of reading material.

Books were a sign of personality. A penchant for crime revealing an inquisitive mind, perhaps, a preference for romance, someone idealistic, or dreamy. Not these books, however, they were just so random, and there was no real order to them either. Books on religion were stuffed in amongst books on politics amongst books on nature amongst books on astrology amongst books on myth and legend. A curious assortment that seemed like it was only for show, the kind you might see in a museum, not one person's library, but a collection added to by numerous people over the years. Generic. Unloved. Forgotten. Certainly, that's what the amount of dust on each suggested. Mel might have liberated at least one volume, but she'd been the only one to do so in an age.

I disturbed the dust with my finger, idly noting motes that mounted the air, acting as frenzied as I had felt when outside. Eventually a title caught my eye. *The Golden Age of Myth and Legend*, faded words carved into brown leather, the author's name beneath the title: Bulfinch. It was familiar somehow, although I was certain I hadn't read it. Everyone, though, knows something of the subject, having been taught at school, perhaps. I needed something to absorb me, and this was it, it would do. Where would I read it, though? There was no comfortable armchair in the library – again a sign that no one tended to visit or indeed linger here – just that stone window seat, which Mel was occupying. I could still feel her staring at me! What did she find so fascinating?

With the book now in my hands, I simply stood where I was and opened it. As I did, several pages fluttered to the floor, those that had come unbound.

"Shit!" I said, bending to retrieve them and stuffing them back into the book, only then opening it further, but in a gentler manner.

There was a foreword on the age of fable, and then stories about various deities, Jupiter, Minerva, Pandora, Apollo and Daphne. It was a hefty book, and there were illustrations too, in pen and ink. A volume that was a hundred years old, it had to be. A treasure. A companion too, something to pass the hours I had to spend here. I could thoroughly immerse myself in it throughout the day, and even the night if I couldn't sleep. And then before I knew it, I'd be on my way back to Birmingham. Safe again.

Safe?

Oh, the thoughts that kept cramming my mind! I wasn't *unsafe* here. Surely?

Still determinedly avoiding Mel's gaze, I located the start of the chapter about Pandora. I knew something about her and the peril of opening a gift she should never have accepted. It wasn't as if she hadn't been warned about it, either. She had, but still she lifted the lid and out of the box flew strife, sickness, toil and other ills, those that would afflict mankind forevermore. The only sprite left that Pandora closed the lid on, was hope.

Oh, the guilt she must have suffered! There was an illustration of her strewn across the casket, her hand lifted to her brow and her eyes closed. The very picture of abject despair.

"A woman to be reviled."

What? Was that Mel who'd said that? Her voice so low it was a whisper.

"Weak."

It was true, Pandora had been.

"Unleashing horror."

Maybe she'd seen what book I'd chosen, had thought about choosing it for herself. Even so, she couldn't have known it was Pandora I was reading about, not specifically.

"Was she punished for the havoc she wreaked? *Sufficiently* punished? Do you think she suffered enough?"

I should really turn to face her, ask her how she knew, and what she meant by it, but my feet were fixed to the spot, my eyes stuck like glue to the illustration.

"Wilful creature!"

Why was she saying all this? Also, why continue to whisper, as if she wasn't on the window seat at all, but had moved from her seat and tiptoed on silent feet across the floor to stand close behind me. I could feel her breath on my neck, not hot but icy cold.

Still she continued.

"The embodiment of evil. The cause of all misery. And all because she couldn't resist!"

This girl was mad, quite mad, saying such things.

"Slaughter."

Slaughter?

"Jason and Medea."

Yes! There was a chapter on Jason and Medea. I'd already noticed that. What was their story? How many had they killed between them?

"So much death."

I looked down at the book, innocuous in its brown leather binding, with its gold carved letters upon it. How I wished I hadn't picked it; hadn't come to the library at all.

"So much guilt."

She was right. Ancient though these characters were, they were guilty of so much wilfulness, greed and jealousy. For them, death was everywhere, waiting around every corner, something greedy too.

I slammed the book shut. There was to be no respite in it. I'd hurry from this room, to my bedroom; there to sleep, just sleep, find relief in that at least.

But Mel wouldn't stop speaking – stop whispering – in my ear.

"There's no way back. No escape. Not once you're here, now that you've washed up on the shores of perdition. Sinful. Unrepentant. A Pandora, a Cassandra. A slayer. No mercy. None at all. Why should there be? Why should you ever be shown mercy again?"

Me?

Every word she spoke, that she hissed, was like a knife that hacked, wounding me, drawing blood, scarring me. This girl didn't know me, and yet the things she was saying! She was condemning me so readily. Was she perfect, though? Because she didn't seem to be. She was as flawed as I was, as the rest of us clearly were. This was an island of imperfection, something in each of the people here that reviled and yet…fascinated me too. People who didn't *pretend* to be perfect, like those in the outside world did, like Caroline and Lorraine, like my benevolent and patronising bosses, like that man on the bus who'd sat next to me, who'd insisted on being so jolly, his grin so wide it could crack his face in half. Like I tried to pretend too. Always smart, always turning up to work early, always aiming to please. A perfect employee. A perfect woman. Praying people believed that. And yet it was all in vain. People *didn't* believe it; the veneer was far too thin.

Unfair! All of it! The world itself was, something dark and turgid and bloody unfair!

I'd started crying again, the well far from empty.

"It's not my fault." My voice was a whisper too, but unlike Mel's it soon grew in volume. "It wasn't my fault. It wasn't. *It isn't!*"

Finally, I swung around, eyes so full of tears that initially they blinded me. The book was still in my hands, and I held it up against me, almost as if it was a shield, warding her off.

"Leave me alone, Mel! Just leave me alone, okay? You know nothing about me. How hard I've tried. I… Just… Fuck off!"

Gradually my sight cleared, my chest, heaving with sobs, calmed.

I blinked and then blinked again.

There was no Mel in front of me. The room was empty, although I continued to look wildly around, my eyes darting all over, examining every corner of the room.

She'd gone, but she couldn't have left so quickly. Could she?

Had I imagined the whole thing, the weight of her stare, and every hateful word she'd uttered?

Chapter Ten

I WAS DESPERATE to get out of the library, feeling as I had in the lift, as if the walls were going to close in and suffocate me. Quickly I shoved the book back on the shelf, noticing something else about it as I did, that hadn't registered before: the edges of it were ragged in places, and if not ragged, then mildewed, as if the entire thing was rotting. Just before I headed off, my eyes scanned the titles closest to it. Not only covered in dust, they were moulding too, a sour smell emanating from them, a stench that filled my nostrils suddenly, made me feel as if I was also rotting, equally as unclean.

I had to find Mel, ask her when she'd left the library, because she *had* been there. That was something I hadn't imagined. She'd been occupying the window seat, staring at me. I wouldn't ask her outright about the whispers, because as impossible as it seemed, and as downright weird, I no longer believed her to be responsible. Someone else had heard whispering, though, through their door at night: Drew, and he'd blamed Tommy, had attacked him because of it. Why? Because whoever had whispered knew the real him, that's what he'd said. And he hadn't liked it, not one little bit.

Oh, this house! I entered one room after another, trying to find some sign of life. Too many rooms, and like the books in the library, no order to them.

Where was everybody? Where was our host? Why did everyone keep disappearing?

A burst of laughter stopped me in my tracks. It came from directly ahead, drifting through more wood panelled walls.

I headed towards the door and yanked it open. Then, as I'd done in the library, I had to blink several times to clear my vision.

It was the living room I'd entered, a fire blazing in the grate at last, flames leaping about, lending some much-needed colour to an otherwise drab room. But did they lend warmth as well? Still chilled to the bone by my experience in the library, I couldn't tell.

Mel was lounging in the armchair, Tommy and Drew opposite her, and on a low table in front of them was a fresh gin bottle. In their hands were glasses every bit as full as they'd been the previous night. Crissy and Peter were absent.

Mel was the first to greet me after taking a huge swig of her drink, ice cubes clinking against each other as she did. Already her cheeks looked flushed and her eyes overbright.

"There you are!" she said, as if greeting someone long lost.

I marched up to her. "When did you leave the library?"

"The library?" She was smiling, but frowning too.

"Yes," I answered. "I was just in the library and so were you."

"Oh, well, we *were* in there together. Briefly."

"So you didn't stay long? When my back was turned, you

just…left?"

Her frown eased as she took another gulp of gin. "That's right, I did. You were so absorbed in that book you were reading you didn't even notice."

"The book of myths and legends," I elaborated.

"Really?"

"Of Pandora, Jason and Medea, Cassandra too."

She laughed. So did Drew and Tommy, who snorted.

"Ok-a-ay." She was clearly unimpressed by the litany of names I'd reeled off.

"You didn't know that, though, which book I'd selected?"

"Why would I?"

Still I persisted. "You didn't say anything before you left either?"

"What like ta ta for now?" How sarcastic she sounded.

"Like anything at all, Mel!"

"Nope. Why would I? Like I said, you were too engrossed in your book."

"You sure? You absolutely sure?"

Amusement faded as irritation took over. "Of course I'm bloody sure!"

"It's just… It's just…"

Tommy interjected. "Hey, Beth, relax. Grab a glass from the kitchen. If you can find the bloody kitchen that is, I swear it keeps swapping places with other rooms." He started pointing. "Try that door there. Just pour yourself a large one, and chill, yeah?"

Indignant, as well as confused, I spun around. "I don't need that kind of help to relax!"

He remained completely unfazed. "Have wine then, if that's your bag. There are plenty of bottles out there. I have to say this for old Petey-boy, he keeps on giving."

"I don't want wine either."

Drew piped up next, a sneer on his lips. "What's the matter? Gone teetotal on us all of a sudden? Gone all saintly?"

"It's early in the day," I retaliated.

"Who cares what the time is? It's Christmas, remember?"

Christmas. Whatever this experience was, it was not that.

Mel had drained her drink and was now leaning forward to grab the gin again.

"Has something spooked you, Beth?"

She'd asked a pertinent question, but not because she cared – there was no shred of empathy in her voice. Rather than answer her, though, I focused on Drew, noting how different his expression was from Tommy's. Instead of slack, there was a tightness to it.

"You said you'd heard whispering."

His expression continued to harden. "Last night? I was drunk."

"This morning too."

He shrugged. "Still drunk, probably."

"Just like you are now. You haven't bothered to sober up one bit."

"So what? Like I've said, we're on holiday, where's the crime?"

His eyes were dark pools, something stirring in them that wanted to bait me further. I was right. He leaned forward, gazed as intently at me as I had gazed at him.

"Best to quit with this saintly act." he advised. "It doesn't suit you at all."

Anger caused my heart to hammer. As tempted as I was to ask him what he meant by those words, I refrained – too afraid he'd tell me. Damn it, but I'd escaped one situation with Caroline and Lorraine, only to walk into another just as intolerable! What did they all know about me? I was a stranger to them; they were strangers to me, even Peter, whatever bond we'd had too long ago to count for anything.

I couldn't stay in that room with them. Let them continue to drink the island dry. Who cared? With a bit of luck they'd all be in a stupor come evening, they'd have burnt themselves out. I could only pray for that result, actively willing them now to drink more and more. The deeper they fell, the longer the climb back would be.

Crissy, where was she? I'd find her instead.

At the staircase, I climbed, one hand on the bannister, feeling not how smooth the handrail was, rather it was cracked in places. I hadn't noticed the roughness of it previously, now though it was obvious, the oak, when I looked at it, more bleached than I remembered. Silvered. As if it was…thirsty. Being bled dry too. I shook my head as I climbed higher. Being here, in this house, on this island, with these people, wasn't good for me. And yet…I'd experienced such peace outside on the headland. Something I'd like to feel again, if I had the chance. Like the proverbial carrot that dangled at the end of a stick, it was that which made me decide to stay – because I *was* considering leaving, going home, and to hell with it, to hell with *them*, but if I could visit the headland again, and I would, I'd spend hours and hours there, then it would be mine again.

What this house contained, however, was far from peaceful. I wasn't comfortable here, wandering through its rooms, ever-changing, as Tommy had suggested, or down the never-ending corridors. The atmosphere too seemed to congeal in places, that's the only way I can describe it, corner after corner heavy with the wreckage of past emotions.

I was in the corridor again, the one where the lights had refused to work, for me at any rate. And despite being daytime, it was dark again, too dark really, considering. What windows there were, at the far corners, offering such little relief.

It was the corridor that would eventually lead to my bedroom. There was no other option but to keep travelling it, backwards and forwards, backwards and forwards, if I wanted to get anywhere, to reach my own so-called sanctuary. Crissy wasn't downstairs to my knowledge, and neither was Peter. Most likely they'd retired up here. I didn't know where Peter's room was, but Crissy's was next door to mine and so I'd knock on her door, have a chat with her, try and get to know her. Timid, shy creature that she was, she might also be my saviour. At least if we stuck together, we could form something of a human shield against the others, draw Peter in too, and even the score, three against three. If luck was really on our side, we could end up avoiding them altogether. There was no need to spend time with them, not really. It might be Christmas, but this was Christmas with a difference. This was Christmas ignored. No rules and no expectations. No need to spend time with Crissy either, really. Even so, I was concerned about her. I wanted to make sure she was okay, and to do that, I had to hurry down this corridor, then another, that with the bedrooms belonging to Drew, Tommy and Mel, before coming to our corridor.

No bloody choice, like I'd said.

I steeled myself and began walking.

What lay behind all these locked doors was none of my business, and neither did I want to know, but if I opened one, just peeped into it, maybe it would…reassure me.

Halfway down the corridor, I stopped, heading over to one of the doors, trying not to think how forbidding it looked, a slab of dark oak that stood guard. Reaching out, I grabbed the handle of the door. Despite always feeling so cold, I was sweating, shaking even. Still, I turned the handle, slowly, so slowly. Part of me desperate to find out what remnants remained of a past inhabitant. Something a little more personal, perhaps, a dress in a wardrobe, a mirror on a dressing table, one with a long, thin handle, framed in mother-of-pearl. Or there could be a photograph in a frame – wouldn't that be something?

My hand stilled. What if there was no evidence of life, but quite the opposite?

I withdrew my hand and held it to my chest as though it were something errant. I couldn't open it, I reminded myself. They were locked, all of them. Why bother trying?

Crissy. She was the reason I was upstairs. I mustn't get distracted.

I continued on, keeping my eyes straight ahead, no longer glancing at the doors that seemed to torment me, that seemed to be…multiplying. Was that it? I hadn't bothered to count them, but there were so many! Drew, Tommy, Mel, Crissy and I were Peter's only guests. He would have mentioned it last night at dinner if there were more people staying, wouldn't he? They'd have been at dinner, surely. And yet, from behind those doors, was that more whispering? Another sound too, a sob, utterly heart-wrenching. I'd already told myself that sounds carried, could it be that Crissy was sobbing, but from so far away?

What if it was indeed someone else, someone broken?

I wouldn't let my thoughts get the better of me, not this time. It had to be Crissy. The poor thing was upset. I'd see what the matter was, and try to console her. Keep my own emotions in check too, not swing wild and untethered from one to the other, at peace one minute, terrified the next, winding myself up, tighter and tighter.

I broke into a run, reached the corner that led to the second corridor, and continued to run, finally reaching our corridor, triumphant about that somehow, that I had managed to. I halted outside her room, my eyes not on her door, not yet, but on the far end of the corridor, where there was no window at all, just another door. Somewhere, as yet, unexplored. Perhaps behind that door was Peter's bedroom, in the turret, the best bedroom of them all, the grandest. It had to be. The master suite.

I could go to his room rather than Crissy's and seize some more time alone with him. I was about to, had taken a few more steps, when another sound stopped me. Not whispering, not sobbing, but singing! It was such a sweet voice, mesmerising, like the call of a siren, impossible to ignore, drawing me to it.

I walked back to Crissy's door. Not locked, not even closed, but ajar.

"Crissy?" I said, opening it further.

Chapter Eleven

APART FROM THE overcoat she'd worn on the journey here, I hadn't really noticed what Crissy had been wearing the previous night at dinner or at breakfast this morning. I don't know why, you'd think I might have done, but for the life of me I hadn't been able to recall it. It registered now, though. She had on a long white dress, over which she'd donned a grey sweatshirt. And she was sitting there in the middle of the room, just like a child might sit, hugging her legs close to her chest, rocking back and forth…and singing.

"Crissy?" I ventured deeper into her room, which contained, like mine, a bed, a chest of drawers, a bedside table and a lamp. Were all the rooms like this? I wondered. As sparse.

I couldn't think about those other rooms now, only Crissy. There was something touching about her demeanour. The innocence of it, I suppose, and such a contrast to the debauchery that was going on downstairs. There was also something so very sad too. As if she was trying to recapture something that was lost.

Even though I was halfway into the room and had called out her name, she didn't acknowledge me. She just continued to rock and sing.

I fell silent, listening to her instead. Felt soothed by her, I realised. Her voice really was crystal clear, familiar somehow, as was the song itself. A melody, sung at night, to ease you towards sleep, to help promote the sweetest of dreams. I found I was swaying too, from side to side. My lips were also moving, silently, my eyes half closed. This place. This strange place. It was possible to feel such unease in it but also such peace.

Somewhere there is sunshine,
Somewhere there is day,
Somewhere there is Morningtown,
Many miles away…

It was as though I was drifting whilst listening, my spirit detaching itself from my body, the house, the island even, and floating above it all, trying to remember…

Had someone sung me this song once? Was that why it was so familiar? A woman I was estranged from, and had been for so many years, my mother, of course. Who else? Crissy's voice was like hers, haunting, making me ache, making me long to feel her arms wrap round me again when I hadn't longed for them in so long, hadn't allowed myself to. The accident. It had devastated her. Devastated us.

But again, that was something I wouldn't think of. As the children in the song were being transported, I wanted to be too, all the way to that true haven, Morningtown.

It was too far, though, always out of reach. Not meant for the likes of me, but for good boys and girls. Hadn't I been good? Hadn't I been innocent? Once. *All* children were. The girl that I was, if only I could remember her. Her smile even, a trace of something. If she'd existed once, would she always exist? Buried deep inside, hiding there.

I wanted to look into the eyes of who I used to be, the eyes too of the woman who'd borne me, to see love there, simple love, not the reproach that I couldn't bear. It scarred me most of all, her shame, her dreadful disappointment. What would I see if I looked into Crissy's eyes right now? Not fear or bewilderment like I was used to, not whilst she was singing like this, but joy for joy's sake, for the sake of a simple lullaby.

Hold on to that, just that.

This moment, it was so unexpected.

I could lose myself in it, fly higher still, far, far away…

Noise. Commotion. It ruined everything, brought me crashing back down to earth, to the stifling confines of this room. Who the hell was it, shouting and whooping in the corridors outside? Screams of laughter that were manic, that hurt the ears.

Anger flared. Why was peace only ever fleeting?

I turned around, towards the door, intending to go into the corridor, to shout at them, Tommy, Drew and Mel, of course, get them to pipe down. Arrogant, ignorant bastards, acting so discourteously in someone else's home, and thinking only of themselves.

I had so wanted to lose myself. If I quietened them, would Crissy start up again, sing another song? One that was equally as poignant?

I'd reached the door, still wincing at the noise the three were making, my head pounding, anger spilling over, and resentment too. *Just shut the fuck up, will you?* I was about to step over the threshold when another sound added to the cacophony.

It was Crissy's voice again, as high as before, but nothing

sweet about it, not this time.

Frowning, I swung back round to face her.

What was going on?

She'd been singing before, her lips moving gently, her body too. She was *still* rocking, but nothing gentle about the movement now. Instead it was feverish, hands like talons digging into her legs. And the sound she was emitting, it was a keening sound, a wailing.

Still on the threshold, I was torn. I wanted them all to stop, longed for silence instead, simple silence. Who did I beg first? Crissy? *Please, you have to stop!*

It wasn't her, though. I had to get away from her, or risk falling into the same terrible despair. If I could stop the other three making such a racket, then maybe, in turn, that would have a knock-on effect. She had to calm down, because that keening, it could crack glass, more than that, your very soul.

I was seething. "For Christ's sake," I said, storming out of her room and down the corridor, to where they were, the three fucking stooges. What was wrong with them? Why didn't they have some consideration? It was only the afternoon, but they were on a rampage already, trying to drag us all down with them. *Idiots!* Peter had to say something too, at some point. This was his house; he needed to lay down some rules.

I was so angry my eyes were bulging, I swear. As I hurried along, my hands bunched into fists. I *hated* the way they were acting, hated them, their selfishness.

"This is out of order, d'ya hear? Way out of order! You can't carry on, disturbing the rest of us. This isn't your house; have a little respect, okay? Stop making such a row!"

As I rounded the corner, I screeched to a halt.

There was no one there. No one hollering or screaming

either. Where were they? In their rooms already?

I went up to Drew's door and banged on it.

"Drew? Are you in there?"

No response.

I then went to Mel's door, and Tommy's, and did the same thing. Tried the handles too, but they wouldn't give. Trying to fathom it, I stood there. It was like someone had just stopped a soundtrack. Were they all on their beds, having passed out already?

I scratched my head. They could have disappeared inside their rooms quickly enough, I supposed, but to quieten like that, when they'd been so loud, so obtrusive...

The silence didn't last for long. More noise started up. Not them, nothing to do with them, but Crissy again, that broken-hearted keening that broke my heart too. What was wrong with her, that pale, nervous girl? That she'd even made it here, to the island, was a puzzle too. She seemed far too fragile. Oh, where the hell was Peter?

He was our host; he should deal with this, not me. Crissy's pitiful cries, though, were something that couldn't be ignored. That *shouldn't* be. She was mourning. But for whom?

"Crissy, don't worry, I'm coming back," I shouted, deciding to leave Tommy, Drew and Mel to it, having no choice really, not if they wouldn't answer their doors.

I ran, surprised at how long it took to reach the corner again, an age.

"Crissy! It's okay, I'm here!"

She wouldn't be able to hear me, not over the noise she was making, but still I called out. As soon as the corner was reached, however, the keening stopped.

Relief surged through me. She was calming down.

Something to be grateful for.

At last, I reached her room. The door was as I'd left it, wide open.

I flew in there.

She wasn't there. She was gone.

I looked all around. "Crissy?"

Where the heck had she gone? A sweet moment had turned into a raucous moment, had turned into this, a kind of oblivion, and all with such swiftness.

My room had an en suite, and so might hers. There was a second door, positioned just where mine was, on the sidewall, and so I crossed over to it, and gently knocked. There was no reply. Testing the handle, it opened, revealing another empty room, as bare as the bedroom. At least I'd littered mine with toiletries, here the shelves were empty.

Frustration replacing anger, I retraced my footsteps back into the corridor, stared down it, to the opposite end, to where I suspected Peter's room might be. Is that where she'd gone? She must have. If she'd gone the other way, we'd have collided.

Perhaps I should go down there too and explore. I might not have been to Peter's room yet, but that didn't mean that Crissy hadn't. Or Tommy, or Mel, or Drew. Only me.

I really should check. But it was so dark at the end of the corridor, and so far away. Plus I was tired. What a day it had been! Full of highs and lows, such terrible lows.

I had to rest. Or I'd never get through the evening. Grab some sleep.

I walked a few more steps, but that was all, just to my room, took the key from my pocket and inserted it into the lock, noticed how rusty the key was, more so than before, a decrepit thing really, and how reluctantly it scraped its way round, forcing back the latch.

Entering my room, my domain, I headed over to the bed, the sheets ruffled, the way I'd left them this morning. I always made the bed at home, but here…I couldn't be bothered. So completely drained, I shed my clothes down to my underwear, and then crawled beneath those creased sheets, my head not only hurting but feeling like it might explode.

Chapter Twelve

CORRIDORS, NOT JUST one or two or three to wander down, but so many. As soon as you turned a corner, thought you were getting somewhere, reaching your destination, there was another, and another. And all of them dark. All of them with room after room on either side. Sounds coming from those rooms, a whisper, a burst of laughter, and crying too.

A nightmare. Part of me knew that's what I was experiencing this time. My brain's way of trying to process all that had happened since arriving on the island. I could try to snap myself out of it, how you sometimes can with dreams, force it to change direction, but the other part of me was curious... What if I just went with it? Saw where it led? Maybe it really would help me make sense of things, although what was it I was trying to understand exactly? These people? With the possible exception of Peter, did I care?

On I trudged down those corridors, my eyes searching all the while, but for what? An open door? There were none, and it was getting darker, the atmosphere as thick as treacle. Just putting one foot in front of the other was becoming a gargantuan effort, like wading through quicksand. I considered turning back but something stopped me… A feeling… Like someone was at my back. Not just someone, but many, those that had stepped out of the shadows, that had been lurking there all along, now becoming bolder.

If I looked back at them, I'd be lost. That's what instinct told me. Because the shadows, although human in form, were not human at all. They would reach out and drag me into the fold, smother me until I couldn't breathe, until I became a shadow too, like them.

I had to keep going through a maze that kept twisting and turning.

I was tiring, though, as exhausted as I had felt before falling asleep. How much longer could I carry on? These corridors were endless!

Stop then.

A voice, a whisper, close to my ear.

Open a door.

Which door? There were so many to choose from.

The right one.

Dreams. They're so bloody cryptic.

Although fearful of what was at my back, I came to a halt, my breathing becoming shallower and my chest heaving.

It was so cold in that corridor, and yet my skin was burning, as if consumed by fire.

I didn't want to do it, open a door, but I'd been curious, hadn't I? About what was behind them? Perhaps it was time to finally lay that curiosity to rest.

Open it!

The voice, the whisper, rasped at me, a command that wouldn't accept refusal.

I'd obey. I'd try. But what if it was futile? All the doors

in this place were locked. Rusted heavy keys needed for each one. Whoever was whispering in my ears, *whatever* it was, would they get angrier still if I failed? What if they reached out too and touched me? I shivered violently, certain that if they did, their touch would freeze me beyond bones through to the marrow, be the thing that shattered my soul rather than Crissy's keening, until I was…what? Nothing. Not even a shadow. I would simply cease to be.

Open the fucking door!

"Okay! Okay!" I said, grasping the handle, icy cold, as I knew it would be.

I wanted it to be locked. I begged for it to be… What was in there, the secret that it held, I didn't want to know. I couldn't. What if it destroyed me?

It wasn't locked. Not in the dream. The catch drew back all too easily, the door opening, no darkness spilling out, but something equally as stark, lurid in its intensity, and white. A sliver of it. Just that, for now… And more whispering.

Trapped.

Deep.

Always.

Forever.

Empty.

Alone.

Shame… Shame… Shame… SHAME!

I screamed. Couldn't listen anymore to the whispering that had reached a peak, that last word also screamed. Such a terrible word. The very worst.

I slammed the door shut; I wouldn't go in there, no matter the voice in my ear. I'd carry on walking that endless corridor, the shadows at my back and only darkness in front. On and on and on and on. Running even… Always running.

The whispering, though, just wouldn't stop.

Shame.

Shame.

Shame.

Shame.

Shame.

In my ears, in my head, going round and round, sobs bursting from me to hear it.

Such a damned shame!

"Oh, there she is! What kept you?"

All five residents in the house, those that I knew of at least, were downstairs in the dining room. It was seven o'clock, time to convene. More's the pity.

The last thing I wanted was to go downstairs, to be with them again, but I was a guest, Peter's guest; it would be rude not to put in an appearance. Plus, I was still concerned for Crissy, wanting to know where she'd gone, and if she was okay. That dream I'd had… It had shaken me to the core. I'd woken like I was drowning, gasping for breath, my hands flailing on either side of me. It was an awful dream, one that I shouldn't have encouraged, what lay behind that door, that strange white light, those words… Time was marching on, it was disappearing, just like the residents of this house seemed to disappear on occasion. For hours I'd slept, right into the evening. Dinner had been at seven o'clock the previous evening, so most likely it'd be at seven today. And I was right.

I entered the dining room, and there they were, Tommy, Drew, Mel, Crissy and Peter.

The three stooges, as I'd mentally dubbed them, were draped over their chairs.

It was Drew who had spoken first, the pupils of his eyes unnaturally wide, making them darker than ever. "Come on," he continued, "enlighten us. Where've you been?"

About to reply, I stopped. I didn't have to explain myself to him, or any of them.

Instead, I walked resolutely to my chair, the same one I'd occupied the previous evening. As I did, I heard Drew's sidekicks snigger. In front of them were more tumblers, full to the brim with gin, the smell of it as sickly as ever. Wine bottles were also open, a couple lying empty on their sides. Pulling my chair out, hearing it whine as it scraped against the bare floor, I eyed Crissy first, then Peter. In contrast to the other two, both were sitting there hunched over, arms pulled in as if trying to make themselves smaller.

I addressed Crissy. "Hey there," my voice was gentle, as if addressing a child rather than a grown woman, "I was looking for you this afternoon. I was worried—"

"She go walkabout, did she?" It was Mel who'd interrupted, as usual showing no concern in her question, only contempt.

"Crissy," I tried again, willing her to look at me, rather than stare at her hands in her lap, but again I wasn't able to continue.

"Walkabout, eh?" Tommy repeated, as belligerent as his cohorts. "Where's there to go on this stupid island? It's not as if you can get lost."

Appalling. And our host, Peter, as subdued as Crissy, failing to reprimand them. What was wrong with him?

What was wrong with everyone here? Because they *were* wrong, and not only them but also this entire set-up, this place where I'd found myself. And what Tommy had just said was wrong too, about not being able to lose yourself here. You could, easily. They did, all the time. Blink and you'd miss 'em. Turn your back, and they were gone. As if… As if the house had consumed them.

Peter raised his head at last, and as he did, I gasped. He was ill, that was obvious to everyone, the victim of some mysterious disease, hence his confinement to a wheelchair, and the weary, pinched look he wore, the lines around his eyes that continued down to his mouth, but now…now he looked withered, his hair even thinner, wispy almost. He was wasting away before our very eyes, as if whatever was responsible was eating him from the inside. The other three, however, seemed only to be growing in stature, were haler, heartier, as if they were sapping Crissy and Peter's energy and feasting on that too.

"Eat," said Peter, distracting me from such unwelcome thoughts. "Please."

Such a plea in his voice, one that made me tremble.

Tommy, Drew and Mel, ravenous as beasts, fell upon the food, what there was of it. Because actually there was no feast in front of us, not like the first night, which had been such a sumptuous affair. Tonight the food on offer could only be described as meagre – cold meats that were pallid, thin slices of equally pale cheese, bread that I couldn't help but think was stale, some pickles and chutneys, and salad vegetables that were limp.

Crissy, Peter and I just watched them. For my part, any appetite I might have had was completely destroyed by their vulgar display. If only they would eat and drink and then retire to another room! I wanted so desperately to speak with Crissy and Peter, only them, but it was impossible. The other three dominated everything, speaking in between mouthfuls, food sometimes spraying from their mouths as they did, gulping down more gin, more wine, talking about Christmas again and what a brilliant time they were having, as long as 'good old Petey' as they insisted on calling him, kept on providing.

"Fucking Christmas," Drew said, laughing wildly. "A waste of everyone's time usually, but this Christmas…well, this one *is* different, this one's good, so good."

"Yep," Tommy agreed, his grin as inane as ever, "good company too." Something they all spluttered at, prompting him to add. "Some of it anyway."

Insufferable. That's what they were. So damned rude. Not for the first time, I wondered how Peter knew people like this. Sweet Peter, gentle Peter, dear and kind, that's what he'd been all those years ago, and now here he was in his house, on his island, one he had thought to invite us to for what looked increasingly like his last Christmas, and these three were spoiling it. Like so many, I didn't much like the season either, had agreed with the sentiment of the invitation – the damned season – that's what had resonated with me, made me want to come here, to experience a kind of *anti-Christmas*, but this…this was too far in the other direction. These three didn't care, not about anything other than themselves. Here, tonight, the food not plentiful, and yet they were devouring it all, stuffing it into their mouths, not noticing that Peter, Crissy and I hadn't yet touched a thing, that we'd go hungry if they didn't stop.

"For fuck's sake, you lot!"

Anger boiled over yet again. So easily it came in this

place. So many emotions… But this one justified. My *actions* were justified.

As well as raising my voice, I found that I had stood up, my chair crashing to the floor behind me.

"You're behaving like animals!"

Crissy spoke at last; she breathed my name. As in Peter's voice earlier, there was a plea in it. *Stop! You have to stop!*

But why did I? What danger was I in? These people, I'd met their type before. Hadn't everybody? They were intolerable. All mouth, all three of them. Shameful people.

Shame… It brought the dream back. The door that I'd opened, the light that had bled out, nothing comforting about it at all. On the contrary, it was the kind of light that struck as much fear into you as the darkness did. And the words that had been whispered…

My anger only intensified, became something wilder.

Without looking at Crissy, without looking at Peter either, I focused only on Tommy, Drew and Mel, their wretched faces, their vacant eyes, their cheeks stuffed full of food still, the mess they'd made, of themselves and the table, their abhorrent indulgence and I began to lift my hand, which was curled into a fist, higher and higher.

How they stared back at me, the three of them, caught in the moment every bit as much as I was – a moment that had deteriorated so quickly, which had been inevitable. Ever since I first set eyes on them, when I knew, I *knew* I didn't just dislike them, I detested them, with every fibre of my being. They were no good, never had been, and never would be. All they were capable of was destruction. And then they'd just walk away.

Before I could bring my hand down, slam it on the table in further temper, there was a scream, and above it the sound of something else, a crack, a splintering.

I turned my head; we all did, not towards the scream, which was Crissy, but the window in its cold stone surround. The middle window, one of three, to the rear of the room, had cracked, and then exploded, Peter having to duck as shards of glass flew inwards. I ducked too, reflexes strong despite my surprise. What was happening? Had the window been struck by lightning? If so, why hadn't I realised there was a storm brewing? It had been breezy earlier on the headland, but only that. Could weather turn so suddenly?

There was glass everywhere, showering the table and showering us, shards, big and small, glistening. The only thing that glistened in this place, almost festive…ironically.

Crissy had screamed *before* the glass had cracked, as if she knew what was going to happen, but then she had quietened. Caught up in the shock of it, I supposed, as we all were, that such a thing could happen. And if there was no storm responsible, then what was? How could glass explode like that? What force was responsible?

Silence. The glass still catching what light there was.

And then came another scream.

Not just Crissy's, not this time. Tommy and Drew were screaming and pointing, too.

As for Peter, he was staring, not horror in his eyes, though, not exactly, but something else. Something I couldn't work out, not in that moment.

Slowly, I looked towards where Tommy and Drew were pointing.

It was Mel.

Mel who was sitting up straight, who was staring, but sightlessly, a shard of glass having embedded itself in her throat, the blood that flowed, in its own way, festive too.

Chapter Thirteen

ANOTHER NIGHTMARE. TWO in quick succession, the second worse by far, and the first had been bad enough. In reality, no window had shattered, and Mel was not dead. But oh, in the dream, how I'd wanted her to be. I'd seen blood pouring from her throat, and I'd experienced triumph. And I wasn't the only one. What I'd seen in Peter's eyes, if not triumph, was excitement. He was actually excited she was dead! He wanted her that way.

I shook my head, trying to purge my troubled thoughts.

I will still in my room, and night had fallen, nothing outside those windows except darkness, tumbling in through the windows, enveloping me in it too.

Using my elbows, I levered myself up into a sitting position and swung my legs onto the floor. Leaning forward, I reached for the lamp positioned beside my bed, a plain lamp, as lacking in personality as every other item of furniture in this house and yet, was that a bad thing? Maybe not, if it had once been filled with people as strange as these.

The light came on, but it wasn't as bright as it had been the night before. It seemed depleted, as if it would soon fail entirely, just keep growing weaker and weaker.

Dinner. I had to get myself ready and join the others.

Make sure Mel really was living and breathing. That Crissy was okay, too, and Peter.

Half an hour later and I was downstairs again, having hurried down those long, lonely corridors upstairs, head down, eyes straight ahead, determination in every step. *Get past the doors, just get past them.* Finding the dining room, I entered. There they were, the five, just as they'd been in the dream – exactly.

"Oh, there she is! What kept you?"

Drew even spoke the same words as he had in that other realm, him, Tommy and Mel lounging in the same positions, clearly having kept their drinking marathon going. As for

Crissy and Peter, they were both staring down at their laps, not even looking up as I entered. Well, I'd make them look up. I'd address them first, ignore the other three if they interrupted, not allow events to play out, break the chain.

"Crissy, hi, how are you? Peter, are you okay?"

Crissy just nodded, refusing to look at me, but Peter raised his head at least.

"Beth, there you are!"

Two things stunned me. The first that he'd said it as if *I* was the one who kept disappearing, the second that, if not aged exactly, like the lamp in my room, he was weaker, what spark there was left in him, spluttering.

As Tommy, Mel and Drew continued to drink, to eat, to help themselves to a meal that was indeed incomparable to the night before, far less inspiring, I noticed other things too.

Crissy was younger than me, and upstairs, when she'd been rocking and singing, she'd looked like a child. Now, though, with her head down, I could see threads of grey in her hair. They kept catching the light. The other three, though, were exactly the same, just as obnoxious, Drew taking a big gulp of wine and then belching loudly, Tommy and Mel dissolving into fits of giggles at the sound. Anger erupted within me, but I fought it back, turned to look around the room instead, observing yet more changes. This was a dining room, at Christmas, and yet I didn't expect or indeed desire for it to be decorated in any way that would reflect the season, damned or otherwise. It seemed we'd all come here intending to escape the faux jollity that this time of year would force upon you – which was fair enough. But this… This was as stark as the rock it resided on. If only there was something to relieve the plainness of the off-white walls, other than several hairline cracks – more than I'd counted yesterday, I was sure of it. Had some appeared overnight? Was that possible? Each corner stood bare, darkness gathering there, nothing more. *Shadows.* There was no…warmth to the room. Decorations would at least have lent it some, even a picture hanging on the wall would have been a concession, or a simple plant somewhere, one of those that are everywhere at Christmas, a poinsettia, that's it, red leaves as soft as velvet. Something else that was living aside from us, *if* this could be called living. Funny to think this was what I'd wanted, but it was a far cry from what I'd thought it would be.

Around me, Mel, Tommy and Drew continued to eat and drink, Crissy touching nothing, Peter doing much as he'd done last night and merely pushing food around his plate. I couldn't eat either. How long I'd be able to sit there, I didn't know. It was excruciating.

Then at last there was change. Drew stood up, swaying a little from side to side. When he spoke, his voice was slurred, my already plummeting heart sinking further to hear it. Clearly, he was priming himself to make an announcement of some sort.

"It's Christmas!" he said, once again belching, his sidekicks once again finding it oh so funny. "Almost. And what do people do at Christmas? They play games, that's what!"

"A game!" Mel was clearly taken with the idea. "Which one?"

Drew looked at Tommy, as if needing help regarding that, but Tommy just shrugged, slurped more gin, and slumped further in his chair.

"Um…" Drew continued, his eyes with that glassy look to them, his mouth lax.

"Charades," I said, I whispered, keen to move the moment on, finding him, and his behaviour, embarrassing.

Mel almost jumped out of her chair with excitement. "Nice one! Love it! I'll go first."

Drew not so much sat as fell back into his chair, nodding at me gratefully. In truth, I was curious – we'd all have to take a turn, surely, what would Crissy and Peter come up with?

Mel lifted her hands, showing it was a film she was going to mime. One word. "Quick fire start," she said, still giggling. "This one's easy." She then opened her mouth almost horrifically wide, revealing both rows of teeth, before clamping it violently shut.

"Jaws!" said Tommy, clutching his stomach he was laughing so much. "Everyone fucking starts with Jaws."

As the winner, he took his turn next. Another film with one word, which was, I suspected, all they could manage in the state they were in. He screwed his eyes shut, held his nose with one hand and with the other waved it up and down repeatedly before sinking down, all of us, even Crissy and Peter, staring confusedly at him.

Abandoning such mimicry, he cried out instead. "It's a disaster, mate. Think disaster!"

"Titanic," was Drew's valiant cry. "It's the bleedin' Titanic!"

"Atta boy!" Tommy congratulated. "Your turn."

Drew declined. "No. No. Can't hack it, mate."

Tommy looked bereft. "But this was your idea!"

"Yeah, yeah, but..." he took another slurp of wine. "Can't think of anything."

"Sure you can," Mel insisted. "Dig deep."

Slowly, reluctantly, he levered himself upwards again, stood for a second, clearly deciding, before doing that whole show reel thing then making a circle with his hands, indicating he was going to act it out in its entirety. "It's one word again," he said, something in his eyes clearing as he focused, becoming steely.

Again, he lifted a hand and mimed pulling something across in front of him – a curtain, perhaps. Next, he ran his hands all over his body, his head back and his eyes closed, as if caught in the throes of ecstasy. One hand reached down towards his crotch, his mouth emitting groans of pleasure now, my entire body stiffening to see it, whereas Mel and Tommy cheered him on. "Go on, Drew! Go the whole hog! Give us some real action."

"Drew," I muttered, but my voice was lost. I couldn't look at him anymore, just kept my head bowed, squirming with further embarrassment.

Drew doubled up in laughter too, having unzipped his pants in what he'd clearly thought was a tantalising manner before zipping them back up again. He then stopped laughing, straightened up and with one hand clenched, made stabbing motions.

Someone whispered the answer. A female voice. Crissy.

"Psycho," she said.

Drew immediately stopped what he was doing and leant forward, both hands on the table as he stared at her.

"What's that you said, Crissy? Speak up, love."

She was silent, hanging her head even lower.

"Crissy!" Drew persisted. "I said speak up. You think you've got the answer, do you?"

Still she remained silent, Peter across the table from me swallowing hard to see it.

"Crissy!" Drew barked her name yet again. "Tell me what you just said!"

I had to interrupt, help her out. "There's no need to speak to her like that, it's just the name of the film—"

"Psycho." Crissy cut across me, not needing my help after all. She'd also raised her head and was staring back at Drew, her gaze just as steely.

There was silence again, a silence that somehow amplified.

Crissy was staring at Drew, and Mel and Tommy were staring at him too.

A tremor coursed through Peter as his gaze swung between the two. Who would be the first to break the deadlock? Crissy or Drew?

"For goodness' sake!" I burst out, unable to stand the tension a minute longer. "It's the name of the film you just mimed, not a personal insult!"

"You sure about that?" Drew replied, his eyes still on Crissy.

"Jeez," I swore under my breath, "and I thought I was paranoid."

More painful silence, and then Drew spoke again. "You won that round, Crissy. Now it's your turn."

Still not faltering, something I was surprised by, that this timid girl was holding her own, she shook her head. "No."

"No?" Another surprise: Drew's bottom lip was trembling. "But you won!"

"No," Crissy continued. "I don't want to play, not anymore."

"You have to. The game's not over yet."

"It should be. It needs to be."

"You have to take your turn!"

"Drew," it was Peter this time, that familiar plea in his voice, his default I was realising, just pleading with us, all the time, to be civil, to be nice, to act like adults not petulant kids. A plea that fell on deaf ears. Even mine.

I stood up, so that my eyes were level with Drew's. He was bullying, and I hated bullies.

"Leave her alone, okay! If she doesn't want to play anymore, that's fine. Nor do I!"

How quickly the mirth returned to his eyes. "Oh really? You don't want to play either."

"I hate games," I said, buoyed by Crissy, refusing to look away, to stand my ground.

"Really?" The shrug of his shoulders was a mockery. "You prefer to gamble instead?"

"Gamble?" What was he talking about? "Just leave it, Drew, okay, don't ruin—"

"Ruin?" His voice rose to an almost hysterical pitch as he threw his arms wide. "What the heck is there to ruin here?"

"Drew." It was Mel who called his name this time, that

unease I'd seen in her when we'd first landed on this infernal island, once again obvious. "Let's me, you and Tommy bugger off somewhere else, back to the living room, play a game between ourselves."

"Chinese whispers!" suggested Tommy, still stupidly happy, seemingly oblivious to the undercurrent that had reached boiling point. "It's better than charades, more fun. Let's all play it! Five is better than three. Let's hear what the voices have to say this time."

Drew, however, just shook his head, looked from me back to Crissy. "Chinese whispers can wait. *This* game isn't over. Crissy, take your turn."

I also turned towards Crissy. "Ignore him," I said. "You don't have to…"

But she was rising, her chest heaving beneath the sweatshirt she wore, beneath the billowing white dress.

"All right, okay," her voice was still so low, "I'll do it."

Drew paused as if surprised, but then he lifted both hands and clapped, a loud booming sound that served not as encouragement but as more of a threat.

I was about to address Crissy again, reiterate that she didn't have to do this, that she was not Drew's to command, and how dare he even think that, when she turned from him completely and fixed her brown eyes solely on me.

During the course of this evening, Peter, Crissy and even Drew had trembled. Now it was me that had shivers running up and down my spine. The way she was looking at me was every bit as determined as the way she'd looked at Drew. Her eyes bore into me as she lifted her hands and mimed.

Three words this time. A film. And it was mine to guess. Only mine. Drew slumping back down, staring at me too. They all were.

With the first word, she pointed to her eyes, not blinking at all.

"I…um…eyes," I spluttered at last. For what else could it be?

She nodded, a slow but definite gesture.

For the second word she carried on pointing to her eyes, but opened them wide, then wider still.

"Eyes… Wide…" I continued, my breath hitching.

The third and final word was coming up, and still she pointed at her eyes, the frown on my face increasing.

In the next instance, she'd shut them, at the same time bringing her hands together in a clap, the result thunderous, making me yelp.

There was no resounding cheer as I spoke the answer, no whooping at all.

"*Eyes Wide Shut*," I said. "The answer is *Eyes Wide Shut.*"

There was more silence instead.

Chapter Fourteen

WHAT WAS THAT? A whisper? Drifting towards me from somewhere in the darkness.

It was late at night and I was in bed. I'd been sleeping again. Now, though, I'd resurfaced. From the moment I had, memories returned, fractured at first, like they are when you first cross that bridge between unconsciousness and consciousness. They were of the evening that had just passed and the game we had played – a stupid game, the kind you'd play at Christmas, that you'd most likely be forced into. Not so different here after all, because once again, we'd been forced into it. It was Drew that had insisted we play, had even taken his turn, but the look on his face when Crissy had guessed the answer! He hadn't liked it one bit. Had taken it personally, as an insult. Pathetic!

And then, as quickly as I'd begun, I stopped in my condemnation of him. For hadn't I done exactly the same? *Eyes Wide Shut.* It was a film I'd heard of but had never seen, like so many films, so many books, so much of everything, there's either not enough time or no inclination. Why the title of it should've touched a nerve I didn't know, but it had, as had the way in which Crissy had stared at me, almost as if she was willing me to guess the answer – and only me.

They'd *all* stared, even quiet, amicable Peter. Why the sudden interest? It was just a stupid title of a stupid film, the result of a stupid game I'd played with stupid people. And yet I hadn't been able to bear their stares, and so I'd turned abruptly and flounced out of the dining room to my bedroom. Running there, down those God-awful corridors, desperate to get away. I'd been intending to grab some alone time with Crissy that evening, and with Peter too, but not anymore. I no longer wanted to speak to any of them – they were all guilty of making me feel so uncomfortable, not just the usual three. All I'd wanted after that was sleep.

But now I was awake. Because of the whispering.

I sat upright, my head turning from side to side in the dark, trying to locate the source of the whispering. It seemed like it was in the air all around me. One minute it was drifting closer and closer, and the next it was so far away, just a mere hint of it. What the voices were saying, though, I had no idea. I couldn't quite catch it. Were the others responsible? All five of them? Were they playing another stupid game? Someone had mentioned Chinese Whispers, Tommy, that was it. It was a game he'd wanted to play. I'd left them long ago, and so what had they done? Brought the game to me? Weird. Fucking weird.

I had to get up and investigate. I didn't want to, though. I wanted to draw the covers right over my head, like I used to when I was a little child, when…

I'd hear voices then too, when I was eleven or twelve, maybe younger, maybe older. Who knew? The past is as much a jumble as this house is. The whispering belonged to my parents. They'd be in the bedroom next door to me, and they'd be whispering to each other, voices low and serious, talking about something that concerned them, that something being me. A sob, sometimes, from my mother, quickly stifled. A grief that didn't shame me, *if* it was to do with me, but sparked something else instead, anger. Anger that rose up in the darkness and ate me alive just as I'd imagined Peter being eaten alive.

The whispering, it had to stop.

I reached for the bedside light, but a fraction before I touched it, I snatched it back. The light would alert them, stop them in their tracks. Instead, I wanted to make it to the door and yank it open, the benefit of surprise mine, all mine, ask them – demand to know – what they meant by this behaviour. Were they trying to frighten me, was that it, all five of them desperate to have themselves some fun at my expense? For what else was there to keep them amused on this chunk of rock? Nothing. There was no TV, only books with crumbling spines, and nowhere to roam, except to the back of the house, to those cliffs…those treacherous cliffs. And yet I longed for them, even in the darkness, for nothing but clouds and sky and sea, and me floating in amongst it, at one with it, something ethereal. Not a part of this world any longer. Not a part of anything…

In the darkness, I stood up, started walking forwards, my hands held out in front of me, like someone blind, trying to balance, to keep upright. I couldn't make out what those responsible were saying, not just yet. I had to get closer.

Just before the door, I came to a halt, strained to hear more, to listen for stifled giggles, too. Tommy, Mel and Drew, at least, outside my door and huddled together.

Except there was no giggling. No one hushing the other as they let loose a burst of laughter. The atmosphere was solemn. So heavy, so intense, that it became the thing to unnerve me, not the actual whispers, but the air of expectation that had built around them.

At last, I could make sense of some words.

Will she?

Won't she?

Nothing.

She'll do nothing.

Shame.

Shame.

Shame.

That word! It echoed in my mind.

If only someone would snigger, so I knew it was them. It had to be, though.

I bolted forward before I had time to think further, determined to expose them, the three, four or five outside my door. Demand they stop, or else…

I was closer to the door than I thought. I only had to reach out and grasp the handle, which I did, my teeth gritted. Straightaway it opened and light flooded in.

Light?

How come there was light? I'd been in darkness before, total darkness. No light from the moon filtering in through the window, and no light beneath the door from the hallway. Yet now there was light. But no further whispering, no joyful shouts of glee either: *Surprise! It's only us! Fooled you, didn't we? Fooled you real good.*

Stark light, the kind I'd dreamed about. And it crept as the darkness crept, into my room, inch by inch, was almost at my toes.

Instantly, I took a step back, my breath stuck in my throat.

"No, no, no." My voice was a whisper now, repeating that one word.

My eyes were so firmly fixed on the light, so intent on making sure it wouldn't touch me that I didn't realise what else was happening. There was a hand at the door.

I gasped. What trickery was this? How were they doing it? It was Tommy, Mel or Drew's hand trying to reach me. It had to be. And what happened when it did, if I reached out too and our fingers touched? Would it pull me forwards into that burning light, roar with laughter yet again as I combusted there and then in front of them, quite the spectacle, a showstopper, the season lit up at last.

Just a hand. Nothing more. Disembodied and coming closer still. My own hands clutched to my chest, but one beginning to respond, to unclench…

Wailing! A keening. The same sound Crissy had been guilty of yesterday. Suddenly it burst into life again. A noise that startled me, that made me snatch my hand back, that made the extended hand judder too, actually judder.

Whatever was going on, I had to escape it. Slam the door and retreat further into my room, back into bed, and do what I'd wanted to earlier and hide beneath the covers until it went away. All of it. Even Crissy, and her wailing, deafening shrieks of despair.

I couldn't help her. Not tonight. I was in no fit state to help anyone.

If this was trickery, it didn't involve her. *If* this was…

I seized the moment, pushed the door shut, my breath still agonised.

Back in the darkness again, I didn't return immediately to bed, I couldn't.

Instead, I sank down where I was, with arms tight around my legs, my body rocking to and fro, just like Crissy had, tears streaming down my face. Again, it took a while to realise something: that there was no need to feel guilty about Crissy, for not rushing to her aid.

Because it wasn't her wailing at all, it was me.

Chapter Fifteen

MORNING BROKE, THE 24th December. Christmas Eve had arrived at last, even here, on Anghyfannedd, the official countdown to the big day. Ah, but my brain, it felt as though it was wrapped in some kind of fog. Some kind of horror. What had happened last night, the whispering, that bleak light, the hand, the wailing. Had it been another dream? A *waking* dream, because I wasn't asleep. I hadn't been since it happened.

I had sat on the floor, wailing – not Crissy, not this time, but emulating her, right down to the way she'd been rocking. I couldn't help myself, couldn't stop either. I'd sobbed and sobbed, loudly, without restraint, and yet no one had checked in on me, certainly not those who had whispered at my door a short while before, the loathsome three, playing a stupid drunken prank, one that had triggered something in me, another tide of emotions.

But now, as early morning rays pierced the gloom, those emotions were spent.

Another two days to get through – *the* days, Christmas Eve and Christmas Day, and then we'd leave. I'd never have to see any of these people again; I could forget them and this island. It had been a mistake to come here, to imagine a refuge, for there was none.

My limbs were stiff from sitting still for so long, having moved from the floor to the bed, but adopting the same position, I groaned as I unfolded myself, shuffling to the edge of the mattress and placing my feet on the rug. What if… What if we didn't stay? We left today. This morning even. By 'we' I meant Crissy and myself, to hell with the others, let them drink more of Peter's wine and spirits, eat his food, act as if they owned the place, it wasn't my problem, I hadn't invited them, Peter had. He could deal with it. Although, I had to admit, there was guilt about that – Peter may have brought this situation on himself, but he wasn't a well man or even perhaps a bad man, just a desperate one. He was fading fast, each time I saw him. A shadow of a man, or maybe just a shadow…

I rubbed at my eyes so hard my vision blurred.

These thoughts…where did they spring from? I needed a distraction, something to take me away from them. I needed a plan.

Crissy didn't like it here. From the moment she'd stepped out of the taxi on the shoreline and stared over the waves at this island that squatted every bit as much as the house did, she'd been nervous. She *hated* it here! I'd caught her crying, in as much despair as I was. We didn't have to stay. We could find that boatman, a man as strange as the island itself, as everyone on it, and beg that he return us to shore.

Christmas Eve. Most people would knock off early from work, taxi drivers included, trains would eventually stop running. If this plan was going to work, we'd have to act fast and leave as soon as possible. If we delayed, left it to later in the day, we truly would be marooned. Crissy had the room next to mine. I could collar her before breakfast and put my suggestion to her, imagining her face as I did, how despair would turn to hope, how *grateful* she'd be. It was a good plan, the deadline spurring me into action. Rising, I made my way to the bathroom. After a quick wash I'd pack what little I'd brought with me. Find Peter too and apologise. Wish him well. Only the best. No hard feelings, not at Christmastime. Some things just weren't meant to be.

Half an hour later and I was ready to leave my room, trying not to think of my reflection when I'd rubbed steam from the bathroom mirror to look. My skin was as grey as this building, no colour to it at all, the circles under my eyes darker, and my cheeks hollow. The creature that had stared back only confirmed to me I was doing the right thing. Being here on the island was taking its toll. There was no way I could stand much more. It was *eating* away at me. The very thing I suspected it had done to Peter, the reason he was in a wheelchair, because this island, and even those he chose to surround himself with, gorged on his life force. What a notion! It was a terrible one. And yet it gained traction.

It took courage to open my bedroom door, half expecting that bleak light to push its way in again, that hand to reach out. Nothing like that happened, of course, it was normal, or as normal as it could be in this place. I entered the corridor and looked behind me, where it trailed into the distance, the winter light from the far window so feeble.

I hurried over to Crissy's door and knocked on the hard wood, began to whisper, to tell her it was me, but then stopped and forced myself to speak more clearly instead.

"Crissy, it's Beth. Sorry if I'm disturbing you. Are you awake? I need to talk to you."

There was no reply. Sighing, I knocked a little harder.

"Crissy, could you let me in? I need a quick word."

Still nothing. Either she was fast asleep or ignoring me. Surely, she wouldn't be out and about, not at this hour. It was barely eight o'clock. Breakfast, when it had been served over the past two days, had been at a leisurely ten.

"Crissy!" I said again, injecting more urgency into my voice. "Please!"

Still nothing, I dared to turn the handle, relieved it wasn't locked, and pushed my way in there, still calling her name, wondering when she'd call back.

With the door fully open, I went inside, my eyes travelling straight to her bed, which was not just empty but fully made up, as if it hadn't been disturbed. Never been slept in at all. Another stupid notion that I dismissed. This *was* her room; I'd seen her in it. And some people were neat…very. She was clearly one of them, as there were no belongings strewn around, nothing that littered the surfaces. Just like she'd never been…

"Stop it!"

I didn't realise I'd said those words aloud, that I'd shouted them, until I heard a voice from behind me.

"Beth? What are you doing?"

I swung around and saw it was Crissy, not in the room, but in the corridor.

"Oh!" Relief surged through me. "There you are."

"Yes, I'm here," she said, as woeful as ever.

I plunged straight in. "I've had an idea. Shall we…um…go into your room, talk about it?"

Her shrug was non-committal. "If you want."

It was what I wanted, but because she didn't move, neither did I. She was so pale. A woman, but a girl too. One

I had to take care of.

I reached out, tried not to notice how hard she flinched as I grabbed her arms.

"We can leave," I said. "Today. This morning. Go home."

"Home?" was all she said in response.

"Yes!" I replied, exasperated. "Look, I don't like it here, and I don't think you do either. It's…uncomfortable. If we find Peter, and just explain how we feel, I'm sure he'd be okay with it. I mean he'll most likely be disappointed, but…too bad." I pulled what was meant to be a doleful expression. "He'll have the other three at least. I don't think there's much hope of shifting them. Leave it to me, okay?" I continued. "I'll sort it."

"How?"

I swallowed. There wasn't even a flicker of excitement in her eyes concerning my plan, as I'd hoped there'd be. "The boatman," I answered. "After Peter, I'll find him."

"What makes you think he's on this island?"

"The boatman? Um…" I was stumped. "I never saw him leave. And there's the boathouse, the very place the boat is meant to be."

"Have you checked?"

"No. Not yet. But—"

"We can't leave."

Despite what she said, I argued on.

"I know it seems like a rude thing to do, throw Peter's hospitality back in his face, and I feel bad about that too, especially as he's…" My voice trailed off. *As vulnerable as you are, as much in need…* That's what I was going to say, but how could I? "Look, we have to leave, that's all I know. This place isn't good for us. You've been upset. Last night,

I was too. There's something about it, it just…keeps getting to me. But I'll sort it all out."

"We can't leave." Again, she said it.

"Crissy, for God's sake—"

She wriggled out of my grip and stepped back.

"I'd like to return to my room now, would you mind?"

"What? Oh…" We sort of shuffled around each other, until she was the one standing in her room and I was in the corridor. "Crissy, I can't believe you want to stay."

"I don't," she said.

Hope flared in my chest again. "Then let me sort it out!"

"We can't leave," she continued to reiterate. "*I* can't. It's too late."

"It isn't! Look, I'm not sure where you live," – she might well have told me, that first night at dinner, but again, due to the alcohol most likely, I couldn't seem to recall – "but I'm from Birmingham. I can't check train times as there's no bloody Wi-Fi on this island, but I'm pretty sure trains run into the early evening. We've plenty of time to reach home."

"You don't know, do you?"

"Know what?"

Again, she shook her head. "You still don't know."

How ironic that she was throwing my perennial concern back at me. I was the one who fretted about what people knew about me, but it was as if there was another big secret, one I was supposed to be aware of. Whatever it was, it didn't matter, not if we were leaving. I wanted to grab her again and tell her this. She was the one who had to understand, not me, but she was already closing the door.

"Crissy!" I shouted instead. "Listen to me. Please."

The door slammed into place.

I was on my own again, with nothing to do but walk the corridors.

Chapter Sixteen

THE WORDS, THE whisperings from last night, reverberated in my head as I walked. Garbled rubbish, because I *had* tried to do something today, to leave here with Crissy in tow, and she'd refused. All that stuff she'd said about it being too late was also rubbish. It wasn't.

I didn't want to traipse these corridors, but I wanted to find Peter next, and so I had to. *My* corridor, where mine and Crissy's bedrooms were, his had to be at the end of it, in that turret most likely, something I'd concluded before, in the master suite.

I'd find him and speak to him, tell him that I at least was leaving, that I was sorry, but there was no way I could stay. Surely he'd understand, wouldn't take offence. It wasn't as if he had sought me out since I'd been here, we'd barely spent any time alone together. If anything, he seemed to have actively avoided me.

The corridor not only ran on and on, it got darker the deeper I ventured into it. Although determined to find Peter, it irked me that I was the one feeling I had to explain when he had so much to explain as well. I stopped, perhaps to bolster myself, looked back towards the far end of the corridor, to where the window was. It was so far away, an extraordinary distance, and yet was that a crack running through the glass, a jagged line from top to bottom? Extraordinary too that I could see it but it was there. Just like the dream, it was getting ready to shatter. A shard of glass impaling me this time rather than Mel, lodging in my throat as it had lodged in hers, blood like a fountain, spraying everywhere.

God, these thoughts! Best to stop staring at the window and get on with what I intended. Keep trekking... *Peter, where the hell are you?*

What a curious house. I knew nothing about it, and yet it must have plenty of history, plenty of people who'd called it home. And now there was Peter. *Just* Peter, who was suffering from some mysterious illness, wasting away. Would someone inherit it after him, another family member? Would anyone *want* to? The thought of being alone here... That was beyond imagining.

At last the corridor was ending, the gloom in far corners rendering them almost black. I hated to look at them, thinking them to be inhabited somehow, some sort of creature there, waiting for me to come closer still. And once I had, it would step forward from the umbra, a twisted, diabolical thing, its body, its features distorted, and it would reach out, as that other hand had reached out, to drag me back with it into the darkness to become something diabolical too. An image so powerful, so terrible, so real, that I almost turned and hurled myself back down that corridor to my room.

Was I safe, though? Even in my bedroom? I'd questioned it before, and I did so again: was anywhere safe on this island? Maybe. On the island's crest, where I'd experienced that feeling of contentedness, of being at one. But at one with what, exactly?

Another door, this one straight in front of me, the walls on either side of it curved slightly. I'd reached the turret. Peter's domain.

Having raised my hand to knock on the door, I stilled. I could hear a noise from inside, a muffled sound, as if whoever was responsible realised someone was listening and was trying to stifle it. Crying. That's what it was. Not the wailing of Crissy or myself, far gentler, although every bit as heart-wrenching. Was it Peter?

The only way to find out was to open the door and peer inside. Maybe I could comfort him somehow, as I'd wanted to comfort Crissy but been unable to.

The door yielded and I stepped inside the room. As I did, my eyes widened. It was such a vast room, much bigger than I could have imagined. The walls were indeed rounded, the kind you might expect to read about in a fairy tale, which a prince or princess might inhabit. Or in the darker fairy tales, be kept prisoner.

Peter was no prisoner; though, this was his home. And there he was, at the far end of the room, with his back to me, in his wheelchair, slumped over a desk there, his head in his arms and his shoulders heaving with the force of his grief.

About to rush over to him, to kneel by his side, ask him what the matter was, I took another moment to survey the room, so intrigued by it. Grand. Yes, it should have been. But like all other rooms I'd seen in this house, it contained only what was necessary, a bed, a side table with a lamp on it, a wardrobe, and the desk Peter was at. Again there was nothing that showed the personality of the man, not even here, in his private quarters. That wasn't what intrigued me most, though. I was coming to expect that. What had caught my attention was the state of the room, the decay that had taken hold. Render on the walls was patchy, exposing brickwork that looked as if it too might just crumble away. The windows in the curve – another set of three - were mottled, cracks in them too, in all the windows of this nameless house, perhaps. Beneath my feet were wooden boards, too worn, too fragile, as if one foot in the wrong place and they would collapse, sending me plummeting through to the floor below. There was also a smell that hung in the air, that of mould, and dust, and grime, the smell of neglect, I suppose, making it hard to breathe.

And in amongst it all was Peter, distraught.

I wanted to console him, to find out what he was crying about. What could possibly be so bad? My feet betrayed me, however, they wouldn't move. I called out instead but perhaps my voice was lower than a whisper as he didn't acknowledge me in any way.

I tried again. Here was a friend, someone in need.

"Peter," I said. "Peter, it's me."

Again, he gave no sign he knew I was there. My only option was to draw closer, not worry about those floorboards, or interrupting him. Although he may well be angry that I'd done so, that I'd stolen upon him, intruded…

He swung round, far quicker than I could have expected him to.

"Beth!" he gasped before I had a chance to say anything more.

I had to find my voice again. "Peter, I—"

"You came."

"To find you? Yes. You see, Peter, I have to—"

"I'm sorry. So sorry."

Poor man, he was clearly so embarrassed. "No, no, please, it's okay. I should be sorry, for barging in on you. It's just… Peter, what's the matter? What's upset you so much?"

"Upset?" He reached up and wiped at his eyes and nose. "I'm okay."

I was stunned that he could deny it. "If you need to talk, Peter, about anything. Well…I'm here. I'm happy to listen."

He wheeled himself closer to me, the tracks of the tears he'd tried to wipe away still evident despite his efforts, his skin as mottled as the glass that surrounded us. I closed the gap by a few steps too, a gesture to prove that I meant what I said.

"Peter, I'm here," I repeated.

"Yes, yes." How sad he looked about that. "You are."

"But those others, Crissy too, I don't know, Peter, they don't seem…" How could I put this without sounding rude? "…your type."

"Oh, they're not. Not at all."

His responses baffled me. "Then why did you ask them here, Peter? To share Christmas with you. Ask me too?"

"Christmas?"

"Yes!" Ill or not, I was growing impatient with the way he was acting. "The Damned Season, remember?"

"Damned? Oh yes, of course. It is. So very damned."

"Peter, are you okay? Really? You were crying and now…" He wasn't making sense at all, just repeating what I said. "Talk to me, Peter, tell me what the matter is, about this house, about those others, why we're here, why you're here. You're not happy being here, clearly. I'm not either. That's why I was coming to see you, because…because…"

I couldn't do it, couldn't continue to say *because I'm*

leaving. This morning. Just as soon as I've packed. Can you notify the boatman? Arrange it?

That I'd hesitated seemed to inject some life into Peter's faded form.

He came closer still, so he could reach up and grip my arms.

"We need to talk, you're right." His words were urgent. "Absolutely right. We *have* to. You're not happy here, I understand that," something that he looked almost pleased about, "but…" now he was the one who faltered as his eyes searched mine, "…not yet. Soon, though. Soon. Oh yes indeed, the time is coming when we will be able to talk."

Somehow, I broke free of his grasp, iron-strong though it was, surprising given his condition. I also took a step backwards, and another, and another. All this despite the fact I wanted to stand my ground. *I must leave. I have to go. Now.*

And yet I couldn't.

Christmas wasn't over. I had to stay.

Had to talk. Soon.

I was running, doing as I'd wanted to do earlier, and flee to my room. I needed a haven. My room wasn't it, though. Or anywhere in this house. I had to go outside instead. There to contemplate, to come to terms with all that had happened so far, the lone encounters with Crissy and Peter, meetings I had wanted, that I had sought to engineer but which had left me more confused, and more sorrowful, than ever.

Chapter Seventeen

I HADN'T BEEN outside since the previous day. Then, there had been a breeze, a light mist that hung over the waters in the distance, but through it you could still see the mainland and the sea that surrounded us, how the waves rolled as they ebbed and flowed. Today, though, the shore and the ocean had vanished.

A sea fret had occurred. A blanket of fog rolling in that obscured everything. Freezing December fog, rendering it colder than ever. I'd wrenched open the front door and was now standing outside in the fret, shivering badly, in need of a woolly hat, gloves and scarf as well as a coat but not wanting to return inside to fetch them, desperate to calm a mind that was becoming feverish.

I walked, my breath expelling yet more mist, little round clouds that hovered rather than dispersed.

No escape. Not yet. Still Christmas to contend with, a flash of hatred, more intense than ever, that the avoidance of this event was what brought me here. That Peter had played upon my vulnerability too, my worry about being exposed, my fear of being alone, even though he hadn't – *couldn't* – have known anything about such fears.

I continued walking, on and on, head down, on

autopilot, trying not to let myself become overwhelmed, thankful for something, that the sea fret would also obscure the house on the way back and I wouldn't have to look into the eyes of it.

If only the sound of seabirds would punctuate this nothingness, their raucous cries so shrill as to be ear piercing. I would welcome it. Anything other than this torturous silence. The only sounds that managed to break through those that caused more distress.

At the rear of the house now, I could feel the ground rising upwards. I tried to measure my tread to make sure I kept well away from the cliff edge, which was not an easy task when you could barely see even a few feet ahead. Not far. Nothing on this island was. It was just a tiny rock in a vast sea, where no one should ever live, not really, and certainly not by themselves. What was the saying? *No man is an island entire of itself,* that was it. We were all connected, somehow, in some way. *I* was connected, to the other five. Being here had made it so. We were parts of a whole.

Profound. Deep. But loneliness in a lonely location encouraged that. There was simply no way to stop the mind from incessantly trying to work things out.

I wanted peace. I craved it. A respite from the questions that plagued me. And there *was* peace here, there was comfort too, in the darkness, even if all too fleeting. Perhaps more peace than in that other world I'd so recently left, that world in which I took a breath, and then another, and existed, nothing more.

Ironic. The whole thing was. My mind like a furnace again.

Where was the spot I'd stood yesterday – only yesterday, although it seemed so much longer than that, just another distant memory. I really mustn't walk much further. Up here, where the island was steeper, the mist was also thicker. It'd be so easy to miscalculate.

I came to a halt, turned round and round, trying to find my bearings and yet succeeding only in making myself more disorientated. Which way now? Impossible to tell. It was as if my actions had eddied the mist, causing it to disperse and then regroup more determinedly. Entombing me. And it was just so cold. No point in continuing. I shouldn't be trying to find peace, not here. That moment before, where I'd felt at one, as if I'd belonged, it was nothing more than an aberration. Rather than look around me, as I just had, I should have simply turned back and retraced my footsteps, gone to the house to seek Peter out again, to explain that I was sorry, really very sorry, but I would not stay.

But the sea crossing, could I make it in this?

Such a short journey, but in these conditions it could still prove treacherous.

Which way should I go? Where was the house?

Damn this mist! And how hard it clung. I couldn't remain static, however, not moving at all. I'd freeze to death. I'd take a few more steps. I'd be careful. So careful…

"Whoa!"

I'd encountered not the edge but a dip of some sort, causing me to tumble forwards, my hands outstretched, my mouth wide open as I screamed.

Just a dip, nothing more. A warning, though. Next time, I might not be so lucky.

I grimaced as I pushed myself upwards, back into a standing position. Lucky? I could talk about being lucky in a place like this? In conditions such as these? It wasn't lucky; it was fucking tragic! To think I'd stood yesterday and gazed over an expanse of ocean and imagined escape. It was a delusion.

I had to get back to the house. There was simply nowhere else to go.

I was blinded again, by darkness, by light, what did it matter? The end result was the same. Again, tentatively, I placed one foot in front of the other, feeling for the ground, my hands held out before me, my eyes straining to see the bricks and mortar which were now familiar to me, which, in the absence of all else, had become my anchor. That house. As damned as the season that had drawn me here. As desolate as the island it was named after. It was in the mists, waiting, waiting, waiting…

Cries erupted from my throat again. No way to stifle them, I had to let them surface, have their freedom at least. Sooner than expected I saw the outline of something hulking, the house, just the silhouette of it, sharp edges softened.

There was no relief on spying it, only increasing dread. What I'd experienced there had been unsettling, untenable even, and yet I had the strongest feeling…

It was nothing compared to what was yet to come.

The day wore on, Crissy keeping to her room for much of it, Peter to his. As for Mel, Tommy and Drew, they occupied the living room, their lair every bit as much as Peter and Crissy's bedroom was theirs. The three of them continued to drink, their laughter drifting towards me now and then, but I didn't join them, kept myself to myself, wandering from room to room downstairs, idling the time away, wishing it would just dissolve.

Back in the library, I tried not to notice yet another crack in the window, and what it may mean. Outside, the fret hadn't lifted – if anything it was heavier than before. Where Mel had sat in the window seat, now I did too, not with one of those ancient books to hand, the binding continuing to unravel, mouldering pages falling to the floor like confetti, I just sat there, my hands in my lap, waiting for the whispering to begin, which it didn't.

The only way to tell that time was indeed passing was to keep checking my watch. There were no clocks in the house, nothing that would aid such a simple endeavour. It *was* passing, though, no matter how slowly, and there was some relief about that at least.

It was Christmas Eve, a fact I had to keep reminding myself of. Also, that I had got what had been promised: Christmas with a difference. Apart from the three stooges getting off their faces at every opportunity, and a stupid game, Christmas had died a death here.

Had I always hated it? The damned season. As I've said, those words had resonated when I'd read them. Even so, had there been enjoyment at some point in my life, that the season had once upon a time elicited? Some spark of childish enthusiasm? Every child looks forward to Christmas, or so we're led to believe, just like they looked forward to their birthdays, something to celebrate, a special day, that reminds us we're special too.

And yet, I couldn't remember if that ever was the case. Not right then, in that gloomy house, in such bleak weather, weather that had conspired to cut us off further. I couldn't recall one ounce of excitement on the run up to the day or the actual day itself. Like this house must have a history, so must I, a fully fledged, rounded history, not something characterised by one thing and one thing only, but that life was as blurred as the edges of the house had been on my approach earlier. I tried to recall, casting my mind back, but I could see only shapes, not as terrifying as those other shapes I'd seen at the windows, not scary at all, in fact. These were ones I longed to see, but how to achieve that? Just like I was cut off from the mainland, I was cut off from them. Adrift in loneliness.

In shame.

Rather than rail against that statement, I simply sat there, too tired to fight. More tears had formed in my eyes, which I hastily rubbed at, as if embarrassed somehow, as if someone was watching me. I turned my head from the window and gazed around the room instead. There wasn't anyone in there. It was just a basic room, a library, floor to ceiling shelves lining two adjoining walls, empty shelves actually, emptier than yesterday. I blinked at that, at the sudden lack. They *had* been fuller, I was certain of it, and yet now the only thing in abundance was the dust that sat upon those shelves, a thick layer of it.

I stood up, still wondering. Had Peter been in here since yesterday, had a clear out of some kind? Also, why had it taken till now to notice that things were changing all around me, not just people disappearing, but physical items as well? Sighing with bewilderment, I crossed over to the shelves, to the tomes that remained, some standing upright still, whilst others, with no books on either side to support them, had fallen, to lie in the dust. I reached out, as I had done the previous day, when the whispering had started, that voice in my ear that I had thought was Mel's, but turned out not to be because Mel had left the room without me even knowing. About to touch one of the books, I hesitated. I had a sudden fear that at my touch the book would crumble, turn to dust.

Where Spring and Centuries Begin... That was the title of the book, a somewhat sad, poetic title, but there was hope in it too, a kind of promise. Familiar too. Had I actually written a poem with a similar title, way back in what seemed like the Dark Ages? New beginnings...maybe that's what the book was about, as well as my poem. I'd had a new beginning. Was in the midst of it, right now. But like Christmas, weren't new beginnings supposed to be joyful? Not something wretched, that had led me here. Was it possible to have more than one new beginning? To *keep* beginning. Until you got it right?

I swung around.

Someone was watching me! I felt that same burning sensation in my back.

"Who is it? Where are you hiding?"

The two walls that weren't lined with bookshelves were wood panelled, right up to the picture rail, and above that was bare plaster, as grimy as elsewhere in the house. There was nowhere to hide, not unless there was a secret door in that panelling, a peephole or two. Not an outlandish theory, not really. A house like this could well have secret paths and passages, the kind where you had to press a catch or something to reveal them. Secrets. This house had so many, the people in it too, and they were welcome to keep them. But if someone was spying on me, playing yet more games, I had to find out why.

My hands got to work, pressing various panels, half fearing the old dry wood would crack like the windows because of the pressure I was exerting. They held fast, though, and yet still I could feel eyes on me, and not one set of eyes either, but several, as if…as if I was a specimen in a jar, something to be observed. Eyes that belonged to that same someone who had whispered in my ear, perhaps, who knew all about me, but which was impossible because no one knew anything about me. Not here. And yet Peter had found me, hadn't he? Earlier I should have asked him how. I still hadn't done so. All the questions I had, everything I wanted to say, just lodged in my throat. Why? His sorry state had persuaded me to stay, but nothing should have. I should have stuck to my resolve and left the island. And yet here I remained, in the library, frantically searching.

The wood panels seemed to be nothing more. I turned to the window again, half expecting to see a crowd of bodies pressed up against the glass, this time on the outside looking in. The cracks giving way under such pressure, indeed the very reason they were there in the first place, because those bodies had stood at the windows before, whenever my back was turned. Unnatural beings. Beings that meant only to harm. And if the window gave way, like it had in my dream, they would swarm in, swarm all over me, leaving me as much of a husk as Peter was.

My body jolted with horror at the prospect, yet still my hands sought to discover. There were no people at the window, of course, but there could be a catch somewhere, on the shelves maybe, behind a book or something, strategically placed. I had to remove every one of them. If they crumbled beneath my hands, so be it.

Book after book was hurled to the floor. Some disintegrated, as fragile as moths, others held firm. There was nothing behind them, though, just bare plaster, as cracked as the windows. Staggering back into the centre of the room, I surveyed the mess I'd made. The mess that others might discover, might wonder at. I should replace the books, not give them more ammunition against me. More reasons to tear me apart. Because they would, given half the chance. Three of them, at least. I was certain of it.

I was still shaking when I tore from the room, left those peering eyes behind me, the whispers that had started up but only in my head, the sniggering, the raucous bursts of laughter, all churning as if in a cauldron rather than my brain. Not real, none of it, imagination and paranoia responsible.

And yet as I found the stairs and took them two at a time, as I fled down those long, dark corridors to my own room, eyes not only remained on me, they *seared* me.

Chapter Eighteen

A FEW HOURS later and I'd composed myself enough to return downstairs to join the others. It was Christmas Eve evening. I couldn't just hide away.

We'd had a feast on our first night here, remnants on the second. Now, though, there was nothing provided, absolutely nothing, and no one thought this strange, no one seemed in the least bit surprised.

As usual, I found all five gathered in the dining room, sitting around an empty table. Three were slumped, the usual three, Peter at the far end, still in decline, seeming barely able to hold on, and then there was Crissy, not slumped, nor apathetic, but gazing at her companions, adjusting her gaze as I entered the room to look at me.

I couldn't help it. I started to rub at my arms, as if I could remove the impression of her stare just by doing so. That second strange experience in the library was still fresh in my mind, and how I'd allowed myself to become so upset so quickly. I wasn't like that ordinarily. It was as though I was in decline, too.

Apart from Crissy, no one acknowledged me as I sat down, the other four locked in their own reverie. Crissy, though, leant forward, her entire manner conspiratorial.

"Don't you see?" she said. "Don't you see yet?"

"See what?" I answered, agitation rising in me again, but anger too, at this entire sorry situation. "What's wrong? Why is there no food? I haven't eaten since… Since…" When had I last eaten? I couldn't remember. On feast night, it had to be. Certainly I'd drunk. But the previous night, and this morning…had I eaten then? Everything was becoming blurred, recent history as well as past.

Still with her voice low, leaning ever closer, Crissy continued to rile me.

"Open your eyes and look around you. Why can't you see?"

My eyes flashed over to Tommy, Mel and Drew – Tommy was sitting up now, his eyes were open but glazed, the usual idiotic grin on his face, and yet there was no mirth in it, not this time, it was more of a rictus grin, something plastered there, set in stone.

Someone yelped. A low sound, but an agitated one. Mel, perhaps? My gaze went from her to Drew, noticing how he shuddered to hear it.

"Drew?" I questioned, but he ignored me.

Again, I adjusted my eyes and looked at Peter. He had his head down, his hands not in his lap but clasped against his chest as if in mortification.

"What the hell's going on?" I rose to my feet. "It's Christmas Eve, and here we all are, at your request, Peter, yours! Why are you all acting so odd? What's wrong with everybody?"

Mel raised her head, eventually looked at me. "Where've you been all afternoon?"

I was incredulous. "Where've I been? Look if this is about the library—"

Drew also lifted his head. "This place," he murmured. "This fucking place." He also rose. "Come on, you two, let's get out of here and leave these losers to it, head to the living room. Come on! Hurry! I have to get away."

There was fear in his voice, I realised, in Mel's gaze too, even in Tommy's forced grin.

"You can't just leave," I said, even though I wanted them to. "It's… It's Christmas Eve!"

Drew bared his teeth. "Fuck Christmas! Fuck all of this!"

He then turned from me, but not before I saw the tears in his eyes, one of them having fallen onto his cheek, to glisten there.

"Drew!" I said, a plea in it, but he was already stalking from the room, the other two in pursuit, Mel sniffing I was sure of it, raising a hand to wipe at her eyes too.

Left alone with Crissy and Peter, I sank back into my chair. Earlier, I'd worked so hard to talk myself into coming down here, to be with them, convincing myself that I'd exaggerated everything I'd experienced to date, because being here, on this desolate island, had played tricks with me. There was nothing splendid about isolation. I couldn't hack it. But I was almost done, nearing the end of my sentence. Soon I'd be free again. Such a short sentence really, when you think about it, days, not weeks, not years, so why did it feel like I'd been here forever already? That life elsewhere was the dream.

Just as Crissy had looked at me, I glared at her.

"What is going on?" I said, I *demanded* to know. Like Drew, I think I snarled.

"Look around you," she whispered, her lower lip trembling. "Just…look."

"I am bloody looking! At the cracked windows, the

cracked walls, the bare table. Peter, I'm looking at you too, and I'm wondering, all the time I'm wondering. What's happening here? This place, what is it?"

When he remained silent, I begged him. "Please, tell me what's going on. How did you find me? How could you have possibly found me? We're alone now, just you, me and Crissy. The other three are gone. It's okay to talk. Tell me."

A bang on the table startled me, made me jump out of my skin.

It was Crissy, pale, fragile, shaking Crissy, more terrified than ever. She had raised her fist and brought it down upon the table, then shot to her feet.

"We are not alone," she hissed. "Don't you understand that? Can't you sense them? Open your eyes! They're everywhere. Everywhere!"

"Crissy," Peter was finally speaking, "wait. It's dangerous. You have to wait."

"Wait till what?" Crissy said. "Till it's too late? I can't! I can't!"

"It's just... It doesn't work that way. You know it doesn't. You can't force this."

"Ghosts!" I blurted out. "Is that what you're talking about, Crissy? Peter, is this place, this island, haunted?"

As Crissy's eyes welled with tears, I focused on Peter. "I don't believe in ghosts, but I know something's wrong here, with this house, with you, with...all of us. This house is affecting us, bringing us down. There are whisperings, I've heard them. Crissy, you've heard them too. The corridors run on and on. There are so many locked doors."

Peter's gaze narrowed. "What makes you think they're locked?"

Of everything I'd said, that was what he'd picked up on.

"I…um…"

"Have you tried them?"

"No, but—"

"Then how do you know?"

"I just…"

"Don't make assumptions, not here."

Again, he was being cryptic. "Why not?"

"Because you'll get stuck if you do, you'll never leave."

Never leave? I had two more days left, that was all. Of course I was going to leave! I was about to say so, threaten to leave now, in fact, that wherever that blasted boatman was, Peter had better get him to prepare the boat. I didn't care that it was so late in the day, that it was Christmas Eve, that nothing was likely to be open back on the mainland. I'd walk to the nearest town if I had to, beg a bed from someone. Sleep in a ditch even. Anything was better than this fucking God-forsaken island.

"Fucking God-forsaken!"

I didn't realise I'd said the words out loud, not until Crissy gasped, her hand flying to cover her mouth.

Immediately contrite, I apologised. I didn't want to upset her further. In that moment all I wanted was to once more protect her, a fierceness in me to do just that. "Crissy—"

It wasn't me that had caused her to gasp, however, or the words that had left my mouth. Her eyes were on the window, the crack in it somehow more prominent, although the leading remained intact. Beyond it, there was only darkness, as blinding as the sea fret from earlier. What was causing her such alarm? It was empty out there. Wasn't it?

Not just staring at the window, she was pointing, and uttering something too, or trying to, the words getting stuck in her throat.

Peter wasn't looking to where she was pointing. Only me. Instead, Peter's head was low again, if not hanging in despair, then something else; resignation.

"Crissy, what's wrong?" I asked, seemed to always be asking. "There's nothing there."

She shook her head, as if in denial. I looked at the window, strained harder to see. Perhaps she was right, and I was wrong. Perhaps she felt like I did in the library, that she was being watched. How could I mock that feeling or distrust her?

"Could it be the others?" I said, changing tack. "Tommy, Mel and Drew? More of their tricks? Peter, for God's sake, why won't you look? Are they out there, do you think? It's just the kind of moronic thing they'd do. Those three are...toxic. Selfish. Arrogant. They're bastards. That's what they are. Complete and utter bastards! Why on earth would you want to spend time with people like that, who only look out for themselves, who take advantage of you? More to the point, why would you force them on Crissy and me?"

I was getting angrier still. My chest heaving, my breath coming in short gasps.

"Why, why, why? Why any of this? It's a nightmare, all of it. A fucking nightmare!"

Crissy had backed away from the table, towards the door. Her lips continuing to move, forcing words out, low and tortured.

"Not a nightmare." That's what it sounded like she was saying. "Real. Too real. Oh God, they're everywhere, all around us. They want to destroy us. Destroy *me*."

I had to calm down and help her. It would be no good if we both lost it. I started walking towards her, intent on doing exactly that, ignoring Peter as he was ignoring us. I'd close the gap, extend an arm to grasp her, not hard this time but softly, to pull her into my arms, to hug and console her. *It's okay, Crissy,* I'd say. *No one's going to hurt you. I'll keep you safe. I promise I will.* I had no chance to utter even one of those words.

She'd looked so scared when staring at the windows, at what she thought she could see, but it couldn't match what was in her eyes when she now looked at me. Not just fear, there was something else, something I can only describe as a realisation. Of what?

"Oh no! Oh no, no, no!"

"Crissy—"

She swiped my hand away, then started running from the dining room to the entrance hall, leaving me so stunned I could do nothing but stand there, watching.

Finally, my limbs started to work again, and I turned to face Peter.

"We have to go after her," I said. "Help her."

"I can't help," was his reply, his head still low, his eyes averted.

I stared at him in utter disgust. "You won't even try?"

"I just… I can't."

If there was to be no help from Peter, then the other three would have to step up. We could split up, cover more ground that way, find her and get to the bottom of what was wrong with her, not be fobbed off again.

After throwing Peter another look of disgust, I too started running, leaving the dining room by a different door, entering the rooms beyond, calling out for Mel, Tommy and Drew. I found them eventually, panic causing me to burst through several more doors, all of them the wrong ones, before reaching the main living room.

There they were, huddled together by a fireplace naked of any flames. It was freezing, and the grate as cold as if it had never once been lit.

"What is it?" I said. "What's going on?"

Three heads refused to look at me. They simply huddled tighter together.

"Tommy! Mel! Drew!" I yelled. "What's wrong with you? Crissy's run off; I don't know where. Get up. Help me find her. We have to find her now."

When still they refused to acknowledge me, I closed the gap between us, hunkered down to their level, and forced them to look at me. When they did, I wished I hadn't been so insistent. They looked terrified, each and every one, but not of something external, the thing or things that had terrified Crissy. Oh no, it was me they were terrified of, just me.

"Fuck you." Spittle flew from my mouth. "Fucking useless. All of you."

It was down to me to save Crissy, only me.

Except I didn't save her. I failed.

Because when I did finally find her, in the boathouse, the otherwise empty boathouse, she had hanged herself. She was dead.

Chapter Nineteen

I TRIED TO cut Crissy loose, but it was no good, I wasn't strong enough. And so I had to leave her there, her legs dangling, that white dress billowing, and retrace my footsteps back to the house, not rushing this time, for what would be the point? She was dead. Stone cold. Something in me feeling like it had died too because of that. I'd hardly known the girl, and yet still I felt that way. All I knew was that she didn't deserve to die. Of all of us here, not her. She was an innocent. She'd known something was wrong, even before setting foot on the island. She'd been full of dread, full of horror, and yet still she had come when she could have refused, got back in the cab and driven away. We all could have.

I didn't want to leave her cold and alone, but it wouldn't be for long. I'd return to the house and fetch the others, drag them out here if I had to, get them to help me free her. Not take no for an answer. Not this time. As for Peter, he'd better get in touch with the boatman somehow, tonight. Christmas be damned, we needed help.

The door to the house was as I'd left it, wide open, the gargoyle that adorned it uglier than ever. For the longest time I stood on the porch and just stared at what was inside, acres of darkness. It took everything in me – *everything* – to enter again, to encounter the strangeness within, but there was strangeness outside too. There was death.

At last, on a deep breath, I went in. Why was it in darkness? Who had gone around turning all the lights off?

"Help." The word left my mouth, but it was like something shrivelled, barely audible even to my own ears. I tried again, but the same thing happened. Maybe it was shock that had rendered me mute. Shock, fear, and disbelief. Crissy was dead. Wasn't she? Taken her own life, hanged herself. Hadn't she? This was *not* what I'd come here for, to witness or experience any of this. And yet here I was, deeply immersed. No turning back. Not now. There was simply no way out of here, not until the boatman returned. *If* he returned.

Which I was beginning to doubt.

I had to locate the light switch, flood this place with light. *Bright, stark light.* Yet I hesitated, not sure that's what I wanted at all. The dark offered much more opportunity to hide. Instead, I took a step forward, forcing legs that felt like they were going to give way at any minute, progressing through the entrance hall, to one of the doors that led off it, entering the maze again, the labyrinth, rooms that kept shifting, I swear it, appearing out of nowhere, then disappearing, just like we all did, here on this island.

I listened as I entered a room, tried to still my breathing so I could hear others breathe instead. There was only silence, as thick as the darkness.

Perhaps it was one of the snugs I was in, one of the rooms that fed off the main living room. An empty room it seemed, as I ventured through it, when surely there should at least be some furniture I'd have to negotiate my way around. On the contrary, I was moving freely enough, nothing but emptiness surrounding me, nothing material that is…

I reprimanded myself. This was not the time to give in to ridiculous fancy! I had to help Crissy, do one last thing for her and cut her free. Afterwards, many questions would need answering, and I wouldn't hold back, not anymore, but right now I had to focus.

Where were the others? I'd left Peter in the dining room. The other three had gone to the main living room. Perhaps I should switch the light on after all…

I inhaled sharply.

Just as it had happened outside, something brushed against me, my arm this time, rather than my cheek, something unseen, its touch feather-light.

"Who's there? Who's watching me? Mel? Tommy? Or Drew, is it you?"

I was sick of their games!

No answer, nothing. But something *had* touched me. It was possible to be mistaken once, but twice? *We're not alone. Don't you understand that? Can't you sense them? Open your eyes! They're everywhere. Everywhere!* That's what Crissy had said, and Peter had told her to quieten down, that it wasn't time to tell me that yet, that it was dangerous to do so. What had he meant by that? What had she meant? Once again, the only conclusion I could draw was that it was ghosts that were everywhere, in the corners, and behind walls and doors. The spirits of those that had come here before and, like Crissy, like Peter almost, had perished. I was being haunted. We all were. What lurked just out of sight breaking free of any restraints that might have been imposed upon them. They'd been nourished over the past few days, by Crissy's fear, by mine, and tonight, finally, by Mel, Tommy and

Drew's fear too.

But it was you they were scared of, remember? The way that they looked at you…

My mind really was veering off track. I was *not* the danger here. But there was danger, of that I was certain, again having to force myself to move forwards, through this carcass of a room, to find another door, hoping, praying that whatever had stepped out of the shadows, had returned there and wouldn't touch me again.

I encountered another empty room, my head spinning because of it. People and objects didn't just disappear. It was impossible. Since the moment I'd stepped onto that boat, along with the others and the silent boatman who'd steered us here, over green, murky waters, it was as if any connection to normality had been severed, like I'd entered another realm entirely, some sort of underworld.

"Mel!" My voice was louder now, desperation lending it strength. "Tommy! Drew! Where are you? Peter. Why are you all hiding?"

It was Christmas again, with no gaiety, no lightness of being, no warmth, no laughter, and no love. And I thought I was fine with that, that I didn't want it anyway. But I *did*. Desperately. My old life back before the accident. That bloody accident!

Anger, on the rise again, obliterated all else, even fear. Good, let it. I'd give it free rein this time, as it would help not hinder me, give me the courage to keep moving, to keep searching. I'd let it flood my body and give me wings.

Picking up pace, I left the room I was in, entered another, and another, room after room after room. And all of them shells. As if everything had been erased. Even the boat. But Crissy was here still, *I* was, and so the others must be too.

I seemed to cover an inordinate amount of ground. The house was big, but not *this* big. And yet I ran and ran in the darkness for what felt like miles, calling out names, and receiving no answer. Peter was no longer in the dining room, and the three no longer huddled in the living room. They must all be upstairs instead, in their rooms. Only Crissy wasn't. She was out there. Swinging.

The tears came, finally, initial shock having receded. Like the waves that surrounded us, I had to ride the crest of so many emotions, and all of them threatening to drown me.

I hunkered down where I was, not just sobbing but howling, like an animal in the wild that had been wounded. Surely the others would hear the noise I was making. It would bring them running to me. It was, after all, enough to wake the dead.

I remained alone, however. Angry about that, tortured by it, aghast, and bewildered.

At some point, I don't know when – time was moving at its own pace again – I dragged myself from the room and somehow found myself back in the entrance hall at the bottom of the stairs, staring upwards. The front door was as I'd left it, open, but the darkness wasn't as intense, it was as if the mist had risen up again, and infiltrated it.

How long I stood there, staring upwards, I also had no idea, but the tears on my cheeks had dried. And I was wearing different clothes. Not jeans and a jumper, but a white dress with a sweatshirt over it. Crissy's clothes. Why was I not surprised by that?

The mist *had* risen, and it was entering the hallway, coming closer. Soon it would reach my feet, which were no longer in boots, but bare. The mist would immobilise me if I let it. Or I could climb the stairs and escape it. Find out what, and who, was up there.

A stairway covered in dust and cobwebs, just as the ceiling of the entrance hall was. As if the house hadn't been lived in recently, not for years and years and years.

I had to decide; the mist was mere inches away. It was too late for Crissy; she was engulfed in it, but maybe not for me...

My hand reaching out, I placed it on the bannister, the wood so rough, so splintered, and hauled myself upwards.

As I continued to climb, it struck me. The night had gone, and morning had broken.

It was Christmas Day. The Damned Season had arrived. Just like it always did.

Chapter Twenty

ON THE LANDING, I looked behind me. The mist had reached the stairs and was also climbing. There was no way back. I was cut off yet again. *Keep going.* More words whispered in my ear, but this time with a hint of encouragement. *Just keep going.*

At the top of the stairs I paused. In front of me was the corridor that I hated most of all, the first one I had to walk down in order to reach Mel, Drew and Tommy's corridor, their rooms, mine and Crissy's too. And, of course, Peter's.

There was something different about it, though. It wasn't shrouded in darkness anymore, so intense. Rather, it was the kind of gloom that allowed me to see.

The doors were open. That was the other difference.

I'd been curious about what lay behind them and had got as far as turning one of the handles, but then I'd stopped, because it was locked. *I'd assumed*, as Peter said.

I still didn't want to see what lay inside them. That wasn't my priority, not yet, I had to find the others, get them to help me with Crissy. Crissy... I looked down at my dress. *Her*s, not mine. Was I honouring her by wearing it, or the opposite? Mocking her?

Keep going.

I would. I'd obey the whispering that had started in my head again, had no choice, as the mist wouldn't let me retreat.

Hitching the dress up, I ran, screaming for the others. "Where are you?"

Here. Here. Look at me, I'm here!

More whispers, but not in my head, something external, coming from the direction of the rooms on either side.

Don't run! No need! We're here! Join us!

Falsities. That's what the whispers were. Mel, Tommy and Drew would be in their rooms, not in these others.

Giggles. Laughter. Low and scratchy.

It is! It's us! Come on, take a peek.

Curiosity can be a wonderful trait, but terrible too if we give in to it recklessly.

My gait had slowed; my head had turned.

A hand, just like there'd been before, at my door, was reaching out. Not just one, but many, many hands. The entire doorframe was stuffed with them. Hands that were clawed, that were gnarled and old, scarred and yellowed, nails bitten to the quick or far too long and curling. Like the mist, they were reaching further and further, desperate to claim me.

Transfixed. Awed. Confused. I was all of that and more. Terrified through to my core. What was this place? What did the mist, and those hands, want with me? The mist would freeze me. Those hands, though, would tear me apart, plunder deep inside and find my heart, my soul, and squeeze them to pulp.

I mustn't hesitate. I had to get past them, keep my eyes straight ahead and not give in to curiosity again. I *was* moving, past those hands, away from the mist, towards another doorway. Why, oh why, did I feel so compelled to look? Not hands, not this time, but faces, piled on top of each other just as the hands had been, eyes bulging and every mouth wide open and screaming – as desperate for help as I was, pleading with me.

No way could I help them, or even bear to keep looking at them.

"I can't help. I can't." Peter's words were now on my lips.

Continuing to run, guilt overwhelmed me, as if their suffering was my fault. As if I'd caused it somehow. Conjured it with my imagination. Spawned something that should have remained behind doors, *locked* doors, bolt after bolt slid into place. I passed more doors, witnessed more suffering, the stark light from my dream spilling out from one just ahead, the door that existed beside it, the only one that was still closed. Somehow that was most terrifying of all. Why did it remain closed? What fresh horror did it contain?

The light was more eerie than the mist, more sinister, that particular door opening wider. My feet had slowed again, despite my brain continuing to yell at me, *Run! Run! Run!* Again, like the dream, voices drifted towards me, compelling me to listen.

Trapped.

Deep.

Shame… Shame… Shame…

"Who are you?" I screamed. "Who's there?"

The light flickered, like the wall sconces had flickered, the only thing to react to my demands. On. Off. On. Off. Enough to drive you mad if you let it. Was that it? Was I mad? If so, it was this island responsible. I'd been sane enough beforehand. Hadn't I?

My body was reacting of its own accord again, taking me towards the door with the light. I swallowed hard, trembling from head to toe. What was in the light, what if it really was worse than the mist, the hands, and the faces? What if it tormented me more? And yet still I drew closer, as stealthy as the mist. If I was closer, I could better make out what the voices were saying. I was sick of riddles, of trying to work everything out. Even so, could I bear the revelation?

It's not time. Not yet. I thought of Peter's words again. What could he possibly mean? Before I could contemplate further, my body doubled over, a pain tearing right through me, causing me to gag, to spew out what little contents my stomach held.

At once the screams of the multitude that filled other doorways became laughter instead, the very mockery I'd feared. *Useless! Useless! Can't help us! Can't help herself!*

I fell to my knees, amidst the mess I'd made, not caring about that, or whether the mist would finally catch up with me, or that the arms would extend further, perhaps the faces too, their mouths opening wider and wider, getting ready to swallow me whole.

I couldn't do this, fight what I didn't understand. My body slumped further onto the ground. I'd lie there instead and await my fate. Give up. It was for the best. There'd be no shame then. Not in death. I'd just close my eyes and drift. Into one of the rooms, perhaps.

A scream! Blood curdling in its intensity. It brought me crashing back, refusing to allow me the luxury of drifting, but keeping me in the thick of the nightmare.

I lifted my head. The scream had come from further up the corridor, a second one following it, a gurgling scream that was suddenly silenced.

"Mel," I whispered. For it had sounded female, high pitched and intense. "Oh, Mel."

I had to rise, get back on my feet and help her, concerned for her, but cursing her too, for preventing me from finding some peace again, a shred of it.

Slip sliding at first, in the puddle of vomit, I soon gained purchase, hurling myself down that corridor, not thinking anymore, only determined to prevent another death.

"Mel, hold on, I'm coming. I'm here."

Her room was just beyond Tommy's, one I was making a beeline for. "Mel! Mel!" Why wasn't she answering me? Where were the other two? They must have heard her too.

The door to her room was also open. Rushing in there, I slipped again, crashing to the floor. It was blood responsible for toppling me this time, crimson in shade, and everywhere, covering the floorboards and dripping down the walls. An impossible amount. The colour of Christmas. And there in the middle of it all, lying dead centre in an empty room, a *completely* empty room, was Mel, a shard of glass in her throat, just as I'd dreamed, both her eyes and her jaw wide open as if caught in mid-scream.

Not suicide, but murder. By whom?

I looked down at my hands and saw how covered in blood they were. As if it was me that had committed such an atrocious act, that was wholly responsible. I shook my head. That wasn't right, was it? It simply couldn't be. It had happened before I'd entered the room. Despite knowing this, I couldn't shake the feeling – that somehow I was responsible for this heinous act. I'd disliked the girl, had actively sought to avoid her, but I'd never wished her harm! The dream I'd had was only that – a dream, something I couldn't control. Just like everything else that was happening.

I couldn't bring myself to step closer to her; it was obvious she was dead. I had to find the others instead. Tell them there was a murderer on the loose, not a ghost, a shadow, or an imagining, but a real person, intent on doing further harm. They were in danger, we all were. Maybe even Peter. There were so many rooms in this house, so many doors. It was entirely possible someone could be hiding behind one of them that even Peter didn't know about. A trickster, someone psychotic, a madman. But Crissy *had* realised, had run down to the boathouse to try to escape, and then, when she'd realised the boat wasn't there…

Tommy – I'd run back to his room. God forbid he was in some kind of drunken stupor, but if he were, I'd wake him from it, take him by the collar and shake him till he surfaced.

The blood on the floor made it impossible to hurry, at least initially. I reached the corridor again and looked towards Tommy's room, and at the mist, a thick wall of it, something intent, and dangerous too.

The killer could be in that mist, could race forward with another weapon in hand. I peered harder. Was there indeed something in it? Something that writhed? Not human but a creature, its jaw as wide open as Mel's, and teeth as sharp as needles?

"Tommy!" I screamed, throwing myself between Mel's room and his, reaching it in virtually one hit, bursting through the open door as I'd burst through Mel's.

His room was empty too. No blood, no bed, nothing except…water, coming from the direction of the en suite and, like the mist, creeping towards me.

"Tommy," I said again, but this time my voice was much

lower, my heart beating faster and faster, dread encasing it.

I didn't want to approach the bathroom, I wanted to turn and run again. I didn't want to because I knew that, yet again, I was too late. But check I must, still hanging on to a glimmer of hope, that I'd be wrong, that this was just another dream, that I'd wake soon.

One step forward, and then another, bare feet becoming wet. This door was also open, but only slightly and so I had to push at it, water rushing over my feet entirely now, water that had once been warm, perhaps, but was now cold, that made me shiver further.

There he was, in the bathtub, immersed. Tommy, with his stupid grin and loping gait, whom I'd also despised. His kind. A follower, a sheep. And yet I hadn't wanted him dead either. But dead he was, drowned. By his own hand or someone else's?

I stepped closer. His eyes were as wide open as Mel's had been, staring just as sightlessly. That grin wiped off his face for good.

Drew. What about him?

I turned from Tommy, tears ensuring my face was as sodden as my feet, as the hem of my dress. Oh, how I wanted to be anywhere but here, away from the grisliness of it all, but worse still was the thought that something might have happened to Drew and to Peter, that I'd be alone with whatever else inhabited this house, at its mercy entirely.

Back in the empty room, I headed straight to the door. Why the room was so completely empty, I couldn't fathom, not right now, but still it niggled, like a worm burrowing in my brain. This had been Tommy's room. I'd watched him disappear inside here, and yet there was no bed, and neither had there been in Mel's room. What did it mean? Any of it?

When leaving Mel's room, I'd checked on the mist, but leaving Tommy's I did no such thing, I ran straight across to Drew's room, where the door was also open, inviting me to burst in yet again. Just another empty room. I had to be quick, ever mindful of that mist, and check the bathroom, but there was no water at my feet.

A quick look, and then it was Peter next. Perhaps Drew was with him already, had sought refuge in the turret. This was Peter's home, he'd know what to do, how we could protect ourselves from what was happening here. He'd better! He'd brought us here, put us in this position. This was his fault! All of it. He'd damned us all.

"You bitch!"

Shock surged through me, replacing anger. There was someone at my back, cursing me, pushing me, my hands coming out in front as I was sent crashing into the wall, only just cushioning the impact. Swiftly, I turned to see my attacker, further stunned when I did.

"Drew!" I breathed. "What are you doing? It's me. Beth."

Teeth bared and eyes wide, something feral.

"Drew," I said again, desperate to make him understand that it really wasn't me he had to be afraid of. "There's someone here, *someone else*, someone dangerous. Mel, Tommy, they're…" I couldn't bring myself to say it. "We have to reach Peter, in the turret. We have to protect him, and protect ourselves too. Drew, what are you doing? Listen to me. There's a murderer on the loose! In this house, on this island. We have to be quick."

Spittle flew from his mouth as he crept nearer, every bit as malicious as the mist.

"You!" he said. "You're the murderer!"

Violently, I shook my head. "No, it's not me, it's not!

Drew, listen, please, we're wasting time. We're in danger. We have to keep running."

As he raised his hands, reaching towards my neck. I pleaded again, but he wouldn't listen. The look in his eyes…it was that of someone that had lost his mind. A psycho, as Crissy had said. The murderer even, having turned on Tommy and Mel, too.

"Drew, stop this. Help me. Please."

"Fucking, fucking bitch!" More spit sprayed my face. "It's you who deserves to die."

As shocked as I was, as fearful, I mined for anger, sought its help again. His hands were just centimetres from my throat. Soon they would enclose it, press harder and harder. I had to get away.

I pushed. With all of my might I pushed, sending him careering back. Stupid fool! He was an idiot, like Tommy, like Mel. Every bit as arrogant as I'd deemed him to be, someone who just wouldn't listen, who followed their own path, who thought they knew better, all the fucking time.

I'd pushed him, and he'd fallen. Before he could rise, I seized my chance and rained my fists down upon him, dragged him back, further towards the wall, grabbed his head in both hands, ignoring the terror in his eyes – terror I'd seen beforehand, downstairs in the living room when he'd looked at me. Did he know? Somehow? That I'd be the one to do this? Had he had a premonition? Had any of them?

It was him or me, that was all I knew. I took his head, and I bashed it against the wall, over and over, tears blinding me and thank God for that, as I didn't want to see yet more blood, the cries that were leaving my throat more than able to cover the cries that left his.

Eventually there were no cries from either of us.

I let go, and his body slumped to the floor. Quickly, I turned away, turned my back on him, ran yet again, across the room and out the door into the corridor, yelped as the mist, so close now, brushed against my skin, as cold as the grave.

"Leave me alone!" My voice was ragged, my eyesight still blurred.

I stumbled from it, staggered at first, but soon picked up speed, running, running, running down that corridor, rounding the corner into my corridor, hearing the window behind me explode, and other windows too, like they'd threatened to do all along. Cracks in walls also became wider, became fissures, and floorboards buckled. At the doors, more hands reached out, more faces screamed, as desperate as I was, mirroring me. At Crissy's room, I was sure she was there, another one who reached out, her feet off the floor, though, and thrashing. At my room, there was only a shadow, silent and watchful.

I ran and ran, hands covering my ears now, on and on, down that endless corridor.

And then it ended. And Peter was there, in his wheelchair, looking as shrivelled and as defeated as ever. But not fearful. I noticed that. There was not one ounce of dread in his eyes anymore, despite all that was happening, the havoc being wreaked.

I came to an abrupt halt as he lifted his head and moved his lips.

"The time has come," he said.

"For what?" I asked, more bewildered than ever.

"To stop running."

Chapter Twenty-One

THE TERROR I'D been feeling, the sheer enormity of it, seemed to evaporate as I continued to stare at Peter, as his words sunk in. I'd travelled all three corridors, had reached the turret. He was right, there was nowhere else to go. Except back the way I'd come.

"You're not alone," he continued. "You never have been."

"I had you," I replied. "Tommy, Mel and Drew, and Crissy too. But... But..."

"They're dead. You killed them."

"No!" Quickly I denied it. "I didn't! Only Drew, and only because I had to. Crissy hanged herself, and the other two were dead when I found them."

"And yet you're still guilty, don't you see?"

My jaw clenched with frustration, I drew closer to him, bent my head so that we were at eye level. "How the fuck can I be guilty, Peter? Tell me!"

His gaze didn't waiver. "You really want to know?"

"Of course I do! What happened with Drew was self-defence. I am not a murderer."

"No, you're not."

"Then how can I be guilty!"

"Walk with me."

He pushed himself up and I was forced to step away from him. On his feet now, he was taller than I expected, and so lean.

"You can walk!" I gasped.

"When I have reason," he said. "Take my hand."

Immediately I shook my head. "We can't go back. Windows are shattering. Walls are crumbling. There are shadows at the door, hands and faces too. The mist is also back there! We can't let it touch us, because if it does…if it does…we'll be lost in it forever."

"The mist has gone." Peter was so calm in the face of my panic, so assured. "Turn around," he encouraged. "It really is time."

Like an infant obeying its parent, I turned, but slowly, not believing him, not quite. Half fancying the mist *would* be there, the murderer too, who wasn't me, it wasn't!

He was right. The mist had cleared, shards of light filtering in through the far window, making the glass that littered the floor glitter like baubles. The doorways too, as far as I could see, were empty, no shadows at them, no kicking feet, or hands outstretched. But the house itself was ruined, a wreck.

And it was this wreck we had to negotiate, as finally I reached out and took his hand.

Gently, he urged me forwards. As our feet crunched over glass and debris, I clung to him, and we continued onwards, past my room, and past Crissy's. We rounded the corner, and I faltered on the approach to the rooms where three bodies lay.

"They're not there anymore," Peter told me.

I denied it. They *were* there. I'd seen them, even if he

hadn't.

"Go ahead and check."

The thought of gazing upon their lifeless forms again appalled me.

"You have to," he continued.

"Why do I?" Again, I was like a small child, every bit as vulnerable as Crissy had been.

"Because they'll haunt you otherwise."

Words as strange as this whole situation. That shouldn't make sense and yet they were starting to… Not the words of a madman. For wasn't the madness over?

It was Drew's room we'd stopped at, the memory of what had happened still so vivid.

"Not him," I whispered. "The others, perhaps, but not him…"

"I'll lead the way," was all Peter said in reply.

Still with my hand in his, we crossed the threshold. I didn't realise I had my eyes firmly shut until he told me to open them.

All that lay before me was a bare room with cracked walls and cobwebs in the corners, long, dark and stringy. No blood. No body. No sign of the violence that had taken place.

My breath left me in a rush. "It wasn't real. Any of it! Just a nightmare!"

When Peter remained quiet, I begged him to answer me. "It is just a nightmare, isn't it? I'll wake up and it'll be Christmas Day. I may not like Drew, or Tommy, or Mel, but we'll spend a nice enough day together, all of us, we'll make the best of it, perhaps have a feast again, like we did on our first night here. And then on Boxing Day we'll leave, go our separate ways. We will do that, won't we? Tell me this is all some terrible dream."

"It isn't a dream," he replied.

"It is. It has to be."

"This is your reality."

"My reality?"

He nodded. "And it will happen over and over. You'll wash up on the shores of perdition each time as if it's the first time, creating your own hell until you finally accept what you did, the agony of it, until you stop running, stop trying to hide from the truth."

The shores of perdition. I'd heard those words before, had read about them, in the library, in that book of myths and legend. Pandora, Cassandra, and now me. Stuck.

"Who are you?" I said at last. "You're not Peter. You don't even look like him! Peter's my age, you can't be the Peter I knew."

"Likely I'm someone you used to know, but in truth, what I am is your last hope."

I stared at him, stared *through* him, if I'm honest, trying to remember. I had known a Peter, a nice boy, kind. He'd worked in a shop. That was where I'd met him. He'd told me about this island and the house that stood on it, that he'd inherit it one day, a lone house on a lonely island, which he had then invited me to for Christmas many years later. Or was the entire scenario as much a myth as those in the book, and Peter a combination of several people, both real and in fiction, as were Caroline and Lorraine, and my benevolent bosses too? And this island, as had just been pointed out, my version of hell.

"You didn't send the invite, did you?"

He shook his head. "And yet still you came, and you brought them with you."

"I did?"

"Yes."

"Tommy… Mel…"

"We can go to their rooms too."

We did, again Peter leading me by the hand, to empty rooms with crumbling plaster and shattered windows, but no bodies in bathtubs or lying on the floor in pools of blood.

"One more corridor to go," said Peter, when we emerged from them.

"*That* corridor," I whispered, where the horror had first begun.

"*That* corridor," he confirmed.

Remembering the starkness of the light that had filtered from one room, what else I had seen in the doorways, the mist that kept track of me, and that other door, the one that had remained stubbornly closed, I grew angry again. "I can't do it. I can't."

His calmness infuriated me further. "So what's the alternative?" he said. "You stay here, *rot* here, like the house itself is rotting, the house that you built."

I was incredulous. "I didn't build this! This is your ancestral home, not mine!"

"You wanted to ask, didn't you, about the history of the house?"

The history? Yes, I had. But I hadn't asked, only thought about it. So how did he know?

"It has no history," he continued. "No name. Nothing. You rebuild it every time you come, every time you step off the boat. The only history this house contains is yours."

I tore my hand from his. "You're going too far now, Peter."

"On the contrary, Beth, we haven't gone far enough."

"You're talking in riddles!"

"Riddles that make sense."

"They don't!"

"And yet you know we need to go to that corridor, that there's a room we can't ignore, not anymore."

I backed away. "No. No. I'll…I'll stay here then, forever if I have to."

"Along with the rest of them."

The rest? "The figures at the window, is that what you mean?" Those that had stared at me, then pointed and screamed. "Who are they, Peter?"

"They're all you, as are Tommy, Mel and Drew. *Aspects* of you. As am I.'

"And Crissy, what about her?"

"The girl you used to be."

"This is nuts, crazy," I continued to protest.

"This time it's also different."

"Different? How?"

"Because you've never made the house this uncomfortable before. You've always tolerated your companions, justified their actions. You've never previously killed them."

"I didn't kill them. I wouldn't!"

"Think about that, Beth. Think hard."

It was the last thing I wanted, but I needed to work out what he was saying. Had I killed them? Driven a shard of glass through Mel's neck, stood back and watched as the blood poured from her, drowned Tommy too, held him deep below the waters, my hands around his neck, me the one grinning inanely? Did I have the power, the strength to do that?

Peter was nodding. "It seems you do."

"But they were dead when I found them, Tommy and Mel at least, and Crissy too."

"Beth," Peter's expression was grave, "they still died because of you."

Tears filled my eyes. "Of them all, I wouldn't have killed Crissy."

Peter looked sad, too. "Sadly, innocence is always the first casualty."

"Peter," I gazed at him through my tears, "you said I rebuild this house every time I come here. Just how many times have I done that?"

"Too many." Again, he took my hand.

"It was an accident, you know," I stuttered, lifting my free hand and dragging it through my hair. "It wasn't my fault. It wasn't intended. None of it."

"And yet so readily you imprisoned yourself."

"I don't know what you're talking about!"

How weary he looked, how old. "*Guilt* is the prison, and it is merciless."

"Okay, okay," I said, growing ever more desperate, "if what you're saying is true. This…this…nonsense… Then I deserve to be here, don't I? In this horrid place, in this house I've built. I'm guilty. And so I should be punished forevermore. That's right, isn't it?"

"You know it isn't."

"Why?" I screamed. "Tell me why!"

"Because you've suffered enough. And so have I, so have Crissy, Tommy, Mel and Drew. We want release too."

My eyes widened further. "You're aspects of me, *what* aspects?"

"We're innocence, stupidity, arrogance, and recklessness. We're also hope."

"Hope?" He'd said that before.

"That's right," he said. "Because hope springs eternal, even in the bleakest of minds."

The tears came in earnest, for Crissy, but also for the others and how I had hated them, *immediately* hated them, aspects of me that had run riot, which I couldn't control.

"But which have finally been laid to rest," Peter reminded me.

"Traits, not people."

"That's right."

"Crissy... I'll never be innocent again."

"You'll be wiser, though."

"More hopeful?"

"If you don't kill me too. Because if you do, then there really is no way back."

Dragging my eyes from him, I turned towards the corner of the corridor.

"What's in the room with the light?"

"Your hospital bed," he answered.

"And in the other room, the one whose door is still closed?"

"Accountability."

Chapter Twenty-Two

THE GIRL APPEARED nice enough, happy, sweet, the kind who could see the wonder in things, the magic. A kid who loved fairy tales, and puppy dogs, and birthday cake, and, of course, Christmas — she'd be breathless with the excitement and anticipation of it. So when did the magic wane, the shine become tarnished, the thrill vanquished? Surliness creeping in, dissatisfaction and resentment. Looking for a thrill still, but of the wrong kind.

Not a kid, not anymore, but young still, younger than me, sixteen, seventeen?

"It's fucking Christmas," the girl said with a sneer on her face. "Again."

Her friend Emily laughed. "Tends to happen this time every year."

"Worse luck," the girl said, still disgusted by the notion.

"Oh, come on, what's your problem?"

"It's just so…boring," the girl spat that last word. "All the grandparents round, aunties, and uncles, everyone stuffing themselves at lunchtime, then falling asleep in front of the Queen's Speech. I can't even escape to my room because Mum won't let me. 'It's Christmas Day,' she'll say, 'come down from your bedroom for once. Make an effort.'"

Emily shrugged. "It's the same in our house, but I don't mind, not really. We get to play games, charades, that kind of thing. Don't you?"

"Charades is the worst, people pick the same films, ancient films from before I was born, always Jaws and Towering fucking Inferno, over and over again!"

"You know what, it's one day, that's all. Why get so upset about it?"

"Because…Because I hate it, that's why. I hate…" The girl clamped her mouth shut, stopped shy of saying 'them', her parents, whom she used to love, but now…

Such anger in the girl, a volcano deep inside that had erupted, an inability to see colours anymore, the world was stark instead, an often brutal place. Parents who were dismayed by her, that didn't understand. 'Where did she go, our little girl?' That's what she'd heard her mother say to her father, whispers that had drifted towards her through the dark one night. 'Why is she always so angry?' The arguments started soon after, because they'd get angry too. 'Don't act like this, don't be so rude, talk civilly or not at all!'

And her mother would cry, something the girl should regret but didn't. It was like she couldn't, her feelings either too hot to handle or numbed.

And the numbness was increasing… That feeling of being so alone. Even with Emily, who did understand her, who said it was just a 'phase' she was experiencing, that it would pass, that it was normal in fact. Other friends also tried to reassure her, but the girl was embroiled in resentment. It was a writhing, squirming thing that fed and fed.

She needed something to bring some colour back into her life, some excitement, especially at this time of year, when everybody but her seemed so fucking happy. Christmas was all about presents, well, she'd treat herself, and treat Emily too…

We'd entered the room, Peter and I, and it was like stepping into another world, one that belonged to this girl, someone displaced in life, and so, so angry.

I looked at Peter, tried to tell him that this girl wasn't someone I knew, but the words wouldn't come – not my words at any rate. Only hers, this girl who was now alone, and lying on her bed, the walls surrounding her covered with photographs of friends, I presumed, most around her own age, one or two who looked a bit older, one boy in particular. All were happy and carefree, like she should be, but wasn't. The girl had a book in her hand, a classic of some sort, was trying to lose herself in it, but she threw it aside in frustration. There were sheets of paper on a desk beside her too that she'd scribbled on, writing down her thoughts, perhaps, her feelings, trying to understand them, but these she ignored. She reached for her mobile instead, her lips forming a smile. One I didn't care for, there was arrogance in it, and spite. And yet…there was an innocence about her too, a sadness. She was a girl who felt she'd lost so much simply by growing up.

This Christmas was going to be magic again. She knew exactly what to get, had heard how amazing it could be, not from her friends, but from others she'd become acquainted with. You only had to put in an order, and it'd be dropped off at your house, deliver-fucking-roo at its finest. It was fun, they said, what everyone did. If you didn't, you were missing out. She'd see colours again, glorious rainbow bursts, the magic that wasn't lost at all. And it was cheap, this stuff, she'd take the money from her mother's purse. By the time she noticed, it'd be too late anyway. Deed done. Emily, though, she could be uptight sometimes, a little girl still, but she could also be persuaded…

It was time she grew up, time they both did. And it'd stop Carla and Lucy from laughing behind their backs at them, which she was sure they did, nudging each other whenever she and Emily walked past them in the school corridor, sniggering away. In the year above them, they thought they were so cool, so superior. Well, she'd show them. She'd impress them.

"Peter," again I addressed him. "I can guess what's about to happen, but this has nothing, *nothing*, to do with me."

Peter remained silent as more images flashed into my mind, came to life all around me. Of course the girl had got what she wanted: the drugs and had indeed enjoyed the respect in those other girl's eyes when she let it be known that she had them, that she intended to liven up Christmas. She had relished that respect, clung to it, at the same time ignoring the trepidation in Emily's eyes, and her words as she begged her to leave off taking them until after Christmas, or better still, flush the tabs down the toilet and not take them at all.

"We don't need shit like that to have fun," Emily had said, a pretty girl, in the bloom of youth, cheeks plump and covered with freckles, dark hair at her shoulders.

"We do," the girl insisted. "We'll take it, you and me, in my bedroom, Christmas Eve."

"Christmas Eve? But I have to be home for Christmas Eve!"

"Not till the evening you don't."

"Early evening."

"Then we'll take it early in the day."

"Look, I'm not sure—"

"You're supposed to be my friend!"

"I am! Your best friend."

The girl shook her head. "Really? Because I think we're growing apart."

"*What? How can you say that? We spend every spare minute together.*"

"*If you were a true friend, you'd want to have a little fun with me.*"

"*I don't think it'll be fun. It'll be…scary!*"

"*Fuck's sake, Emily, it is fun! It only lasts an hour or two anyway. You'll be fine for the evening. This is my present to you. You can't say no! Christmas with a difference. That's what this'll be. Something to remember. When the old folks start turning up it'll make us smile, the memory of it, when we have to be on our best behaviour again, all day, and all bloody evening, not say a word out of line, not say a word at all actually, that's what they'd prefer. We'll be able to hug it to us like a secret, our first trip together, the first of many!*"

"*Your mum and dad, though—*"

"*They're out, till the evening. They won't know a thing. Emily, you have to do this. We do. Certain people are going to want to hear about it.*"

"*I don't care about those people.*"

"*I do, though.*"

"*You shouldn't, they're just… They're using you.*"

"*Look, if you don't want to, fine. Let's forget all our plans over Christmas, forget…us.*"

"*Don't be like that! It's just, I don't know… I really don't.*"

The girl, though, wouldn't let up. She kept on and on at Emily. "You have to. You can't let me do this alone. I mean it, I won't be friends with you anymore. I won't."

Bitch. A total bitch. Just a kid.

I truly didn't want to see anymore but couldn't stop the images from forming. This room we'd entered, the only closed room in the corridor, was where the true horror lay.

The girls had taken the drugs, Emily still so nervous, the

185

other pumped with excitement. Then Emily relaxed, began to laugh and giggle as much as the girl, the pair of them becoming euphoric, not frightened at all, but enthralled, feeling invincible, beautiful.

Beauty that all too soon shifted and changed, that grew darker.

"Oh God," I uttered, knowing how dark it could get.

The expression on Emily's face was no longer beatific. It began to twist and turn, she started to shake too, to cry out for the other girl, begging her for help. But the girl didn't listen because for her there was still beauty, colours that dazzled, and a sound in the air like the tinkling of bells. Emily's screams couldn't break through.

"Help me! Help!"

Not just shaking, Emily's entire body was juddering as she fell to the floor, her back arched, her head too, her mouth open, still screaming but silently, nothing leaving her mouth now but a sickly white foam that kept on bubbling.

Eventually, the girl stopped swaying. "Emily? Emily, what's the matter? What's wrong?" Her friend's eyes had rolled in her head, and her jaw was slack.

"Emily? Are you okay? Emily!"

She dropped to her knees, held her friend as her final breaths were wrung from her. The effects subsiding eventually, stark reality returned, her heart now banging in terror against the walls of her chest, thump, thump, thumping away. This world, she couldn't bear it without her friend in it. She couldn't return if Emily was gone, if she was dead.

"Are you dead, Emily?"

Oh, this girl! She really expected an answer! Emily, though, was limp in her arms, eyes open and staring but at nothing this time, just an empty void.

"Emily, it's Christmas! Our best ever, remember? You can't be dead."

But she was, and there were tabs left. Tabs that the terrified girl reached out for, swallowing another, then another, reasoning that this was all illusion, a good trip turned sour. More might do the trick; bring back the fun, and Emily too. They would solve everything. Make it all right again. Because that's what the tabs did, she'd been told that, by her other friends. It had to be true. She'd make the nightmare stop.

One way or another.

As Emily had collapsed, so now did the other girl, the girl called Beth…

The room had been in gloom before, but now lights as bright as in that other room flooded it. Whispers too, from two figures that were no more substantial than smoke, dressed in white, like angels, but of the human kind, and with their heads together.

Not who you'd expect.

Not the usual type.

A good home…loved.

The parents…

Desolate.

Does nothing. Doesn't respond.

Trapped.

Trapped deep.

Miracles happen.

Does she deserve one?

Of course!

Did this to herself.

Yeah, I know.

Killed her friend.

The drugs did.

Her idea, though.
Harsh.
Harsh? Why?
She's young.
Still guilty.
We all make mistakes.
As big as this?
You ever done drugs?
What? Well…
I have. In the past.
Really?
We've been lucky.
I hear you, but…
But what?
Not sure I believe in miracles.
It's Christmas, though…
The damned season.
Yeah, it's busy.
Kids like her.
More and more.
What is it about Christmas?
Expectation. Boredom.
It's like a disease.
It is.
Shame.
Terrible shame.
Her second Christmas…
Too long. Just… Too long.
A shell. Empty.
Alone.
You know what?
What?

Still love Christmas.
Really?
My little boy does.
You got a kid?
He's crazy about it.
Not jaded?
Not yet.
Good, that's good.
Something to be grateful for.
Come on, let's grab some food
Yeah, we'll check back later.
What is it?
It's just... What if she's always trapped?
Forever?
Yeah.
Don't dwell.
Hold on to hope, eh?
There's always hope. Hey.
Hey what?
Damned season or not, Happy Christmas!
Happy Christmas!

Happy Christmas... Happy Christmas... Happy Christmas...

The voices, the figures, faded at last.

Chapter Twenty-Three

"I'M NOT DEAD."

"No, you're not."

"But this is hell?"

"Yes. It is."

"Oh shit! Oh God! What I did was terrible. I *do* deserve to be here."

"And yet look around you, the house is crumbling further."

Peter was right. In the room where we were standing, there weren't just cracks and fissures; there was a gaping hole! A crash resounded, elsewhere in the house, the sound of more destruction, of bricks tearing themselves loose.

Beneath me, the ground was beginning to shake, some kind of earthquake, throwing us hard against each other, my arms reaching out to cling to Peter as I'd clung to him before, hands closing around his arms as I begged him to get us out of there.

He had to shout to make himself heard. "Where would we go?"

"What? I don't care where! Anywhere but here."

I screamed as the ground shifted yet again, certain it would soon give way beneath us.

"Peter, come on!"

"You have to think where it is you want to go."

"I don't understand what you mean!" When he remained silent, I screamed again. "Why aren't we moving?"

"Think, Beth! Think!" His voice was as urgent as mine.

Desperately I tried to appease him. "The boathouse! We'll go there."

"There's no boat."

"Well, where is it? It's the only way off this island!"

"Is it? Are you sure?"

Another rumble, deafening, as if one entire side of this structure had collapsed, the other side bound to follow suit.

I sobbed. "I don't know! I don't know where to go!"

"You do."

"I'll work it out later."

"Work it out now!"

"If I'm not dead, I will be soon!"

"Either that, or you'll keep coming here."

"There's nothing here!"

"You'll rebuild it."

Like he had said I would, over and over.

"Oh, Peter!" I was clinging to him, but he was no more substantial than the two figures whose heads had been together, who'd been discussing me at my bedside. If he faded too, I wouldn't keep washing up on these shores, I'd drown instead or be buried beneath the rubble of my own destruction. Looking into eyes that begged me, I began to realise.

"The sea. The cliffs. We have to go there!"

Something in him lit up, it brought him back to life.

"Let's go," he said, finally moving, pulling me along, out of that room and into a corridor that was filled with dust now, as thick as mist, and threatening to choke us.

"Quick," I said, coughing and spluttering. "We have to be quick."

Devastation. Annihilation. A tearing down of the walls I'd built, that I'd sought shelter in. Days I'd been here, just days… And yet as I once more raced down that corridor, as Peter kept pace, I remembered thinking how time dragged here, how it felt infinite. In truth, how long had I kept coming here, trying to find another aspect of me? Courage.

This corridor! It was taking too long to reach the end, to find the stairs. We never would at this rate.

"Bring it to an end!" Peter demanded. "Bring it to an end or you're right, we'll die."

"I'm trying!" I called back, also screaming as something from behind just missed me, a door torn off its hinges, voices protesting, a chorus of them, begging for release too.

"What about them?" I asked.

"Them you do bury, and you bury them deep. They're demons, every one of them."

"Demons?"

"Your demons. Now, bring this corridor to an end!"

The stairs! There they were.

"Look! Look!" I said, pointing. "We've done it."

We reached the top of them just as there was an almighty roar behind us, those we were leaving behind not ready to release their grip.

Rather than eye the stairs, we both looked back, and as we did, I noticed that Peter, like he'd done when he was in the wheelchair, was folded in on himself, as flimsy as paper.

"NO!" My roar was a match for the destruction around us. "We are getting out of here!"

I had clung to him, but now, as I reached out to him, he

clung to me, and despite the treads buckling, the staircase swaying, trying to break loose from the walls, to shake us off, we got down those steps, we took them two at a time, *we flew*.

They did indeed break loose, collapsing along with everything else, that warren of rooms which was ever changing, ever multiplying, finally perishing. We were at the bottom, and the door was in sight, and open, blessedly open, the new day a special day after all.

Still dragging Peter along, noticing that his feet moved faster the closer we got to the door, we threw ourselves over the threshold, there to land in a tangled heap.

"Quick! Quick!" I continued to urge. There was no time to rest, the house was the thing folding in on itself now, the gargoyle, another demon, screaming, its mouth twisting in protest, its eyes bulging. We had to get clear of it.

We scrambled to our feet, ran further, only stopping when we'd reached a safe distance.

Rubble. That's all it was. This grand house of many rooms and many corridors.

For the longest time all we did was stare, both of us, I think, trying hard to believe what we were seeing.

"Why a house?" I said at last. "Why an island?" Anghyfannedd – a place of desolation.

"You'd cast yourself adrift."

He was right, I had done, long before the drugs.

"Emily," I whispered, stricken. "What if she washed up somewhere like this?"

"Impossible."

"Why?"

"She wasn't guilty."

"Where is she?"

"Somewhere far better."

It was that I'd continue to cling to, that belief.

At last we reached the crest of the island where I'd previously felt a degree of peace, the *only* place, not just soothed, as I was soothed by Crissy's singing, but a far deeper serenity than that.

"Here," I said, as we came to a standstill. "This is where I need to be."

For a moment we simply stood there, staring outwards. No hint of a mist, not even on the horizon, and the sea was blue, birds circling each other, coming closer and closer.

"Beautiful," I breathed, my eyes misting with tears. No need for enhancement, it was enough. *More* than enough.

I turned to Peter. "Eyes wide open," I said. "I can see now. Perfectly."

"But you have to accept."

"It was an accident," I insisted. *Just* an accident. "But an accident that was my fault."

Closing my eyes briefly, a sob escaped. On opening them, I took in yet again the beauty of my surrounds. I knew what I had to do. Before that, though, there was one more thing I had to get straight. "The girl was Beth, *I'm* Beth, but I'm not the Beth that I believed myself to be. I'm not twenty-six, I've never lived in Birmingham. I'm not estranged from my parents either, a loner, living in a flat, or rather not living, not with any real purpose."

"The road not taken," Peter said, as enigmatic as ever. On seeing my confusion, he relented. "You could have been that person, if you'd carried on the way you were. As angry, as reckless—"

"And as stupid," I said. "I was spoilt, a rebel without a good enough cause, looking for something when I had everything, attaching blame where I shouldn't, forgetting about the simple things in life. The magic. It's everywhere and at all times of year."

"If you learn, though, if you evolve, you can honour Emily in that way."

"Tommy, Mel and Drew are dead. I won't be resurrecting them, I promise."

He smiled and it was genuine rather than pained, reaching his eyes.

On a deep breath, I spoke again. "I have to jump, don't I? Off this cliff."

"I believe it's called a leap of faith."

"Will you jump with me?"

A bellow of laughter startled me.

"Peter?" I said, finding myself smiling too, also for the first time in as long as I could remember. Oh, but he looked so much stronger now. He sighed before giving a slight shake of his head and looked back to where we'd come from.

"I should stay."

"But why? If you don't return with me, then—"

"There'll be others."

"What? Here? On my island."

Again, he roared with laughter. "The house is yours, Beth, not the island! Others will wash up too, construct a story, a reason, just like you did, saying I invited them, when I didn't, building a world around them, one that could be even more terrifying than the one you built, far more treacherous." He stopped smiling then and paled a little. "I can't say I'm looking forward to it, but it's what I do, what I'm here for. Without me, the demons truly would take over. There'd be no escape at all."

"No hope of it."

"That's right," he said, not an old man at all, but young and handsome, like a prince.

I leant forward, couldn't help myself, and gently kissed his lips, relaxed into him as his arms then came round to hold me, the two of us, on that cliff edge, embracing like lovers.

"Will I remember this?" I whispered.

"Maybe."

"Will I remember you?"

"What's in my heart is now in yours."

"The road back won't be easy."

"It's a long journey, but acceptance, strangely, makes it easier."

"And hope."

"That too."

"If only I could rewind it all."

"If only."

Tears blurred my eyes again. "I'm sorry about Emily. So very sorry."

"You need to be."

"She was my best friend."

"Then do right by her. Find a way."

He released me and took a step back.

"It's time," he said, and his voice was an echo, merely that, coming from far, far away.

I turned to face outward again, noticed yet more blue in the sea and in the sky, more birds soaring, listened as waves lapped against each other, gently, not raging at all.

Imagining that Peter's hand was still in mine, I took a step forward.

Went home for Christmas.

A note from the author

As much as I love writing, building a relationship with readers is even more exciting! I occasionally send newsletters with details on new releases, special offers and other bits of news relating to the Psychic Surveys series as well as all my other books. If you'd like to subscribe, sign up here!

www.shanistruthers.com

Made in United States
North Haven, CT
30 October 2021